AN ADDISON ROMANTIC COZY MYSTERY
- BOOK 3 -
CABIN BEWARE
WELCOME TO SHADOW LAKE CAMPGROUNDS
PAT HUNSICKER

CABIN BEWARE
An Addison Romantic Cozy Mystery Book 3
Copyright © 2020 by Pat Hunsicker
All Rights Reserved.

ISBN 9798559891279

This book is a work of fiction. Although the places mentioned may be real, the characters, names, and incidents and all other details are products of the author's imagination and are used fictitiously. Any resemblance to actual organizations, events, or persons, living or dead, is purely coincident. No part of this publication may be copied, reproduced in any format, by any means, electronic or otherwise, without prior consent from the copyright owner and publisher of this book. The only exception is brief quotations in printed reviews.

Written By Pat Hunsicker

Cover Design By Marina Yakubivska & GCreative

Dedication

A special thank you to my Husband for the printers, paper, ink and all his support. But most of all, his patience.

My Beta Readers:
Joya, Jerry, Ruth and Kelly

My Editor:
Donna

The President of the Writers Group:
Kora

My Family & Friends: Thank you all for taking the time to read and review my third book- Cabin Beware; and offering all of the helpful advice. I love you all.

Table of Contents

Chapter One

Harper Gray was sitting at her kitchen table, doing what she does best, making a list. She and her boyfriend Harrison Roberts are going to spend a week in a cabin up on Shadow Lake. It's about forty-five minutes north of Addison, New York.

The cabin has all the essential equipment. The living room has a fireplace, a small kitchen with a stove, refrigerator, microwave, and all the cookware anyone could ever need. It has two bedrooms with all the sheets, pillows, and blankets. It is almost like a hotel, you can get maid service if you pay a little extra, but there are only two of them, so Harper elected to make their bed and do their dishes.

They leave on Saturday, which is in two days. She is getting so excited.

All of a sudden, Harper's back door opens, and she hears, "Yoo-hoo." It's Liz Sketcher, Harper's best friend and neighbor. They even look alike. They both have long blond hair, blue eyes. Liz is 5'4" tall, and Harper is 5'6" tall. They're only a couple of years apart. Harper is thirty, and Liz is thirty-two. They get along great. The two girls have never had a fight or crosswords with each other. Liz is the manager for Harper over at the Main Street Drug Store.

Long story short, Harper inherited the store when her older half-brother Jack Carpenter, was murdered in the square; he left everything to Harper.

Harper didn't know how to run a business, but Liz has worked at the drug store for years, so Liz now runs the place for Harper. There are also four apartments above the store that Harper owns.

"Liz, I'm so glad you are here, I'm making my list for the lake, and I need to know when you and Tom are coming up, and will you please spend the night? The cabin has two bedrooms. We can spend the day on the pontoon boat we rented, then have a cookout and later dessert by the fire pit. Please."

"Oh, Harper, you know we will be there for the whole day and night. We are going to have so much fun.

Tom said we could come up on Wednesday and leave early Thursday since he has a new job starting."

Tom owns his own construction company; he builds houses. He even has a couple of guys that work for him.

"Wait until you see the lake, we will be going to Harrison's famous Turtle Cove. It's great; the cabin has a dock right out back, so we don't have to drive over to the marina to get the boat each day. Did I tell you there is a grill out back and a fire pit? We can get wood right at the campgrounds."

"Do you have to cook all your meals? Didn't you say there was a restaurant nearby?"

"There are a couple of restaurants close, but the first night we are there, I want to make a romantic dinner. Maybe have Harrison grill steaks, and I'll make baked potatoes and a salad. Oh, and don't forget the wine. When you guys come, I have planned a special dinner. We have to use the grill and later the fire pit for our dessert. You're going to love it."

"Tell me, what are we having?"

"No way, it's going to be a surprise."

"Okay, Harper, back to reality for a minute. You need to come by the store today or tomorrow and sign our paychecks for this Friday and next Friday. The bills are all caught up, so the week you're gone will be a breeze. The store practically runs itself. Between Nate, Renee, Tonya, Henry, and Paul, they all have it covered. We have a great crew."

"I'll stop by after I go grocery shopping. Now that I have the menu planned, I still have a few things to pick up."

"Is there anything you want Tom and me to bring?"

"Of course not. Just remember your bathing suits; Harrison said no skinny dipping in the day time."

"He does take all the fun out of everything; it must be the police officer in him. Well, I better get to work, or my boss may fire me."

"No, I'm your boss, and there is no way I would fire you. I'll see you later."

Liz headed to work and was thinking, *I wonder what Harper has planned for dinner. It doesn't matter; whatever she makes will be great. She is such a great cook and a great baker, even though neither she nor anyone else received the blue ribbon at the country fair. That was a horrible day. Harper had entered the pie contest at the country fair. It was a Caramel Pecan Pie. Three other ladies made and entered a pecan pie. Nettie Kline, Megan Elizabeth Miller, and Missy Jane Clarke. One of the judges Katie Dunlap who used to be a contestant, was a judge this time. One of these ladies knew that Katie was allergic to cinnamon. That's what did her in. But leave it to Harper, she cracked the case wide open when she got the suspect to confess.*

Harper checked her list one more time, then headed out to the grocery store. *I know I'm buying too much food, but you know the way Harrison eats. It'll be fine. We'll cook a couple of times and maybe go out a couple of times.*

After the store, Harper stopped at home to drop off all the food. Then she headed back to the drug store. As she entered, she thought to herself. *Please let's not have any problems next week; no one is allowed to die. The last time someone died was Helen, who was eighty-seven years old and lived upstairs in one of the apartments.*

She had a heart attack while taking a bath. The water ran over the tub, made its way to the store below, and ruined some of the merchandise. Tom came to Harper's aid and fixed the ceiling and floor in the store that was ruined and the bathroom floor in Helen's apartment.

Harper walked into the store, she greeted Nate and Renee and then headed to the back to say "hi" to Henry. Harper went to the office to sign the checks. Liz had everything ready for Harper to sign. There were a couple of boxes stacked up beside Liz's desk. "What's in these boxes?" Harper inquired.

Chapter Two

"Oh, those boxes came in yesterday, but I wanted to wait for you before I opened them."

"Well, what's in them?"

"Remember when you asked me to check into some products that have our name on them. I finally found a company in Cleveland, Ohio, that can put any logo on anything we would like."

"Come on, let's open them," Harper said impatiently.

They started pulling out all kinds of things, T-shirts, mugs, key chains, pens, even baseball hats. They all say, "Addison, NY." The girls were so happy. There was a little bit of everything and in all different colors.

"These are wonderful. We can put the new merchandise on an end cap somewhere upfront, so people know we have them. I know we don't get a lot of visitors, but maybe some of our residents would like to send them to family members, grandchildren. Think of the possibility."

Liz declared. "Look, they even sent a catalog. Maybe next time we order, we can find some other things. If these are not what our customers want, they'll tell us what they would like to see."

"Liz, you did good; have the girls help you stage them. I need to get home and finish packing. If you need anything, just call me."

As Harper was leaving, she ran into Kay Sanders, a friend from college, and an author who had moved here to write her seventh book. She rented one of Harper's apartment above the drug store.

"Hi Kay, how are you doing? I wanted to let you know I will not be going to the Inspiring Author's Group this Saturday. *That is our writer's group held every other Saturday at the library.* Harrison and I are going away for a week's vacation. How is your book coming?"

"The book is coming along just fine. I sit over at the square when I need some inspiration. Can I ask you, something Harper, would you like to be one of my beta readers?"

"Are you kidding me? I would love to. Wait, what does a beta reader have to do?"

"You read the story and fix any words that I have misspelled or any punctuation marks that I put in the wrong place or didn't put where they should go. Even mark a sentence that doesn't make any sense to you."

"Oh, I can do that. You are working on your seventh book. I doubt you have made very many spelling errors or left out any punctuation marks."

"You would be surprised. I get to typing, and sometimes my brain goes faster than my fingers. All the wrong letters come out; I do have a program on my computer called Spelling Correction that I run the chapter through that helps put the punctuation marks where they should be. Still, it doesn't pick up words that I spelled wrong. Like when I type HER, my fingers always end up typing HERE. This program doesn't pick up on stuff like that. That is why I need human eyes, my beta readers. I have five chapters ready so far.

"Kay, are you busy right now? I haven't had time to talk to you in a while. Do you have time to go over to Rosie's Diner and grab a cup of coffee?"

"You must have read my mind, that is where I was going. But first, let me go get you the first five chapters, so maybe you can read them while on your vacation."

When they entered Rosie's, there were the towns three gossip ladies. Nettie was the ring leader, her twin sister Zoe and their friend Marge; they just agreed to what Nettie says. Harper said, Hello to the ladies. Nettie turned and faced the other direction like she didn't hear Harper.

Harper just shook her head and thought. *What did I ever do to her to make her dislike me so much?*

Apparently, Kay had not come across these three yet. She wanted to know all about them. Harper did the short version. Nettie accused Harper of killing Jack. Then when Nettie was in jail for poisoning one of the judges at the country fair. Nettie blamed Harper. Of course, Nettie left out that Harper found the real killer and got Nettie out of jail. She knows everything you say, so be careful. Harper warned Kay.

"I have a t-shirt that I should wear around that woman Nettie, it says. Be careful, or you might end up in my next novel," Kay quoted.

Harper just laughed.

It felt good to sit and talk to Kay for a little while. Harper promised to get together when she and Harrison got back from their vacation. With Kay's chapters in hand, Harper headed home.

She wanted to go over the menu again to make sure she had everything. The cabin has all the utensils and cookware but no spices or condiments. She reminded herself to take her knives and a cutting board.

<u>Saturday Night</u> – Steak, baked potato, salad, beer, and wine. Steak seasoning, salt, and pepper, butter, sour cream, lettuce, tomatoes, salad dressing.

<u>Sunday Morning</u> –
Coffee, Baileys, bacon, and french toast.
Cinnamon, butter, eggs, milk, vanilla, sugar, Texas toast, and syrup.

<u>Sunday Lunch</u> – Roll ups for the boat. *They are so easy to make. You take a piece of lunch meat, put a piece of cheese on top of it, and roll it up. I usually take some kind of mustard to dunk them in.* Lunchmeat, cheese, honey mustard, bottled water, packets of lemonade and iced tea, pickles, chips, cookies.

<u>Sunday Dinner</u> – Hamburgers, corn on the cob, Caprese salad. Buns, ketchup, mustard, red onion, butter, basil, tomato, mozzarella, balsamic vinegar.

<u>Monday Morning</u> – Go to the restaurant in town for a huge breakfast.

<u>Monday Lunch</u> – Roll ups for the boat. Same as Sunday lunch.

<u>Monday Night</u> – Chicken on the grill, green beans, scalloped potatoes, apple sauce. Chicken breast, one can green beans, bacon, sugar, vinegar, a box of scalloped potatoes, butter, milk, apple sauce.

<u>Tuesday Morning</u> – Coffee, Bacon, Eggs, Toast Bread, Butter, Jelly.

<u>Tuesday Lunch</u> – Chicken Sandwiches with grapes. Can of chicken, grapes, celery, mayo, croissants, and chips.

<u>Tuesday Dinner</u> – Go out to a nice restaurant.

<u>Wednesday Morning</u> – (Liz and Tom are here.) Coffee, Sausage Gravy, Biscuits, Hash Browns. Sausage, milk, flour, can of biscuits, frozen hash browns.

<u>Wednesday Lunch</u> – Roll ups, snacks, brownies Lunch meat, cheese, pickles, snacks, brownies

<u>Wednesday Night</u> – Chicken Hobo Dinners, Salad. Chicken, red potatoes, butter, one pkg.

ranch dressing, cheddar cheese, bacon, parsley, foil, cooking spray.

Wednesday Dessert – Peach Cobbler. Char-coal, Dutch oven, oil, two cans peaches, one box yellow cake mix, butter, one can 7-up, one can whip cream.

Thursday Morning – Take Liz and Tom to the restaurant for breakfast.

Thursday Lunch – Pinwheels. Cream cheese, ranch mix, milk, bacon, deli lunch meat, burrito tortillas.

Thursday Night – Flat Bread Pizza. Flatbread, pizza sauce, shredded mozzarella cheese, pepperoni.

Friday Morning – Whatever is left.

Friday Lunch – Whatever is left.

<u>**Friday Night**</u> –

Mac and cheese in crock-pot, hamburgers on the grill. Macaroni, a block of cheddar cheese, one can evaporated milk, butter.

<u>**Saturday**</u> – Have to leave for home.

Okay, Harper is a little obsessed with lists. But if she didn't, she would be making peanut butter and jelly sandwiches for every meal.

Harper's house was a mess. She and Harrison had piles of things everywhere. Stuff for the boat. Her clothes for a week. The crock-pot, the Dutch-oven. Non-perishables. Her knives, the cutting board, cheese grater, corkscrew, and bottle opener. A cooler set out for the food that needs to stay cold.

She looked around and thought are they going to need a truck to get them there.

Harrison also had piles—his clothes for the week, fishing gear, tools.

Friday came and went. Harper could hardly sleep that Friday night.

She was up early Saturday morning. Ready to go. Harrison got to her house around seven o'clock. Harper was putting all the cold food in the cooler when Harrison walked in. All the other piles were sitting there, waiting to be packed.

Harper had gone through each pile again and took some of the stuff out. Even her clothes, she cut down a lot. She decided she only needed a couple of bathing suits, one cover-up. Some shorts and tops and one sun-dress.

Harper got smart and loaded the spices and non-perishables in the crock-pot and some stuff in the Dutch-oven. That helped with extra space.

The car was packed, and they were ready to get out of the driveway when Harrison looked at Harper and said. "Are you ready, Roy?" Her reply was, "I was born ready." This is what they said before going on any big trip, just like their parents used to.

Chapter Three

They were finally on their way. Harper couldn't stop talking. She was making more lists out loud about what all needs to get done when they get there.

- Go to the cabin first, unload.
- Drive over to the marina to get the boat.
- Harrison drives the boat back over to the cabin dock.
- Harper drives the car back over.
- Make their lunch.
- Harrison can load all the stuff on the boat while she makes lunch.
- Get on the boat and head to Turtle Cove.
- Dinner is steak on the gas grill, with baked potatoes and a salad.

She wanted their first night to be extra special.

Little did Harper know, but Harrison also had a special night planned. He had a little black box in his pocket. So, tonight was the perfect time to pop the question. They had been dating for over a year. His career with the Addison Police Force was going well. She was the girl of his dreams. He loved her so much. He thought he would wait until after dinner to ask her to marry him if he could wait that long. That box was burning a hole in his pocket.

As they pulled into the campgrounds, the first stop was at the office to get the key to their cabin. They were in number thirteen. Thirteen is Harper's lucky number. When they drove up to the cabin, there were police cars everywhere. They both looked at each other, like what is going on? The guy at the office didn't say a word about all the police cars.

They pulled into their parking space. Harrison and Harper both went over to one of the officers to ask what was going on. The officer stated that this is a crime scene; they found a body inside cabin fourteen.

Other spectators were standing around, so while Harrison was questioning the police, Harper was asking the people standing around questions. All they knew was it was an older guy. They thought he was one of the handymen around here. He did the small repair jobs around the park. Why he was staying in a cabin, no one knew for sure. No one seemed to have a problem with him. Most people stay to themselves while here on vacation. I mean, when you pass someone, you say "Hi" but you don't get up in their business. This guy had a dog with him. People heard the dog barking, and someone called the office to report it. Next thing they knew, police were everywhere.

The coroner showed up, and they brought the body out.

Harrison came over to Harper and said. "They have a mess on their hands—one old guy who was beaten up bad. Someone wanted him dead. Whoever it was, they did a number on the guy. They must have used a baseball bat because his head was smashed in."

"Do they have any suspects yet? Did they tell you the guy's name? What's going to happen to the little dog?"

"Harper, you do ask a lot of questions all at once, don't you? No, they don't have any suspects yet. The guy's name was Howard Martin. You were talking about a dog. No one said anything about a dog."

"The people I talked to said a dog was barking; that is why they called the office. When they took the body out, the little dog was sitting by the front door. I don't remember seeing him leave, but he must have since he isn't here any longer."

Harrison insisted they leave. "Come on, Harper, let's get unpacked and start our vacation. Try and put this bad experience out of our minds. We are here to have fun and not get caught up in a murder."

That is what they did. Harrison and Harper unloaded the car, got most of the stuff put away, put on their bathing suits, and headed to the marina to pick-up their pontoon boat. Harrison drove the boat back to the cabin's dock while Harper drove the car back. She started making lunch, little meat and cheese roll-ups. Harper grabbed some snacks and water. She was ready to go. Harrison was loading all the boat stuff. Towels, floats, a radio, the cooler that Harper had packed with all the food. They were ready to go.

As Harrison backed out of the dock, Harper saw the little dog sitting over on the bank of the lake. He looked lost. She thought, *you poor thing; you lost your good buddy. I'll remember to put some food out tonight for you.*

The weather was the best. It was sunny but not too hot. When Harrison and Harper arrived at Turtle Cove and put the anchor down, it was time to jump into the most refreshing water. They had been so busy hurrying around all morning, and now it was time to relax. So, that is what they did. They each got on one of the rafts and floated around. Harrison, the smart one, tied each raft to the boat so they wouldn't get too far away. Harrison's dad used to secure the rafts he and his sister were on in the same way. They played some more, then climbed aboard to fix some lunch.

While they ate, Harper went on and on about the little dog. "Wonder what his name is? Who is going to take care of him?" *Also, on her mind was Howard Martin. Who was he? Who killed him, and why? She*

The rest of the afternoon, they played in the warm water. Even though Harper had put sunscreen on, she was getting a little red. Harrison said they should be getting back. They have all week to play in the great lake.

Harper started talking about how she could hardly wait for Liz and Tom to get here on Wednesday. They are going to have a ball.

Harrison said. "Do you think those two will ever get married?"

"Of course, they will. I have never seen two people, so in love, except maybe you and me."

Chapter Four

While Harrison covered the boat, Harper added, she would run and get her shower. While she started on dinner, Harrison could get his shower. She needed to take the steaks out to rest, put the potatoes in the oven, and make the salad. The wine and beer were already chillin' in the fridge.

Harper went to find her list with the menu; she needed to hang it up so she could remember what she had planned for each day. She also found Kay's book she was going to read, and thought, *I'll take it on the boat tomorrow and read some of it then.* Tomorrow's breakfast is bacon and French toast. Dinner is Hamburgers, corn on the cob, and Caprese salad.

Harrison came walking out of the bedroom, all nice and clean and smelling good. Harper couldn't resist going over to him and hugging him and thanking him again for bringing her here.

Harrison asked. "How long before I have to start the grill?

Harper told him. "The potatoes have about thirty more minutes, and everything else is ready. I just need to set the table."

"If you don't need me, I was going to go set up the fire pit for later this evening."

"Oh, that sounds fine. Would you keep an eye out for the little dog? I was going to give him some food. Only if he could talk and tell us what happened to his master, poor thing."

Harrison gave Harper a funny look *like you need to stay out of this murder investigation.* She saw it and just turned her back to him.

"Okay, I think you could light the grill and start the steaks."

The steaks were perfect; the potatoes were soft with butter slathered all over them; the salad was cold and crisp. Everything worked out great. They were getting ready to do the dishes when the little dog showed up at their front door. Harper ran over and opened the door; the dog came right in. She didn't eat all of her steak, so she cut some little pieces for the dog. Harper pulled down two bowls, one for some water and the other one for the food. The little dog ate the steak so fast she didn't even think he swallowed. Harper didn't want to give him too much to eat; she didn't want him to be sick. "I'll give you something else later." Harper was checking the dog for a collar; he thought she was just playing. It was too cute. He had a collar on with his name; it was Ruddy. They played with Ruddy for a little while, then he went to the door and sat. He must have to go out after that steak. Harper opened the door and let him out.

Harrison came over and hugged her. "You are the best human being, I know. Harper, you worry so much about that little dog. You are too much." Harrison then got down on one knee and pulled out that black box he had been carrying around for the past week and said. "Harper Lynn Gray, will you be my wife?" With tears in her eyes, of course, she said YES. He put the ring on her finger; it was the right size, thank goodness. What an excellent start to their first of many vacations together.

Harrison had fixed the fire pit so they could have a fire tonight. As they sat around the fire, Ruddy laid there with them. Harper could hardly keep her eyes off the new ring on her finger, and saying over and over again, "Harper Lynn Roberts, Harper Lynn Roberts."

It was time to turn in; they had had a busy day.

Harper questioned. "What should we do with Ruddy?"

"It's nice out he can stay outside. He'll be fine."

They said good night to Ruddy and headed to bed, but two minutes later, they could hear Ruddy crying. Harper couldn't stand it; she went and let him in. Harper refilled the water bowl and told Ruddy he had to sleep on the living room floor, not the couch. It was like he understood what she was saying, and he laid right down on the rug.

They woke up to scratching on their door; of course, it was Ruddy who needed to go out.

Harper got up and let him out and started the coffee. Harrison came out and gave his fiancé a big hug and a kiss. Harrison said he would uncover the boat while she started breakfast. Harper put the bacon in the oven and made the coating for the French toast. She put the syrup in the microwave to warm up. By the time

Harrison came back, everything was ready. Ruddy followed Harrison in the cabin. He was ready for breakfast too. Harper gave Ruddy one piece of bacon and some of the French toast. He ate it all.

After they did the dishes, Harper went to get her bathing suit on, and then she made the roll-ups for their lunch. While Harper got everything, ready Harrison went to the office to buy some ice for the cooler.

They were ready to get on the boat, but there sat Ruddy. He was such a good dog. He was just a little runt of a thing. He was a mutt of some kind. Harper and Ruddy looked at Harrison with their big eyes, and she asked. "Can we take him with us?" Harrison gave her and Ruddy a look then said. "Okay, come on." Harper was so excited, and Ruddy stood there and wagged his tail so fast. Ruddy wasn't afraid of the boat; he climbed right on, jumped up on a seat, and waited for them to take off.

It was Sunday, and as they headed to Turtle Cove, there were boats everywhere. Some of them were tied together so people could jump from one boat to the next while partying. Everyone was having fun. They slipped past all the boats, and Harper asked if there would be a lot of people at Turtle Cove. Harrison told her probably not because people like to stay out in the lake to water ski or tie their boats together to party. No one came back to the cove. You might see one or two boats, but they never stay long.

After they anchored the boat, Harrison jumped in while Harper asked how's the water. All he said was wet —N*o kidding, smarty pants!*

Harper sat on the side of the boat where the ladder was and dipped her toes in. It was a little chilly, but she was sure once she got in, it would be fine. In she went. Ruddy stood there watching them when Harper came over and told Ruddy. "It's fine; come on in." Ruddy stood there for a minute, wagging his tail then jumped. He splashed Harper; all she could do was laugh. Ruddy swam around and out to where Harrison was lying on a raft. When Ruddy got there, Harrison picked him up and put him on the raft with him. Harper went back up the ladder to get her phone to take some pictures. Then with her raft, she got back in and swam over to Harrison and Ruddy.

They swam and laughed a lot; Ruddy was trying to walk on the raft. That was a sight!

It was time to get out and dry off and maybe have a snack.

Chapter Five

Harrison lifted Ruddy out of the water and handed him to Harper to get him back on the boat. After drying him off, Harper got out all the food. She was glad she put in some paper plates and bowls. Harper fixed Ruddy, a bowl of water. Harrison put a couple of roll-ups on his plate and a bag of chips. Harper set a plate for Ruddy with one of the roll-ups taken apart. Otherwise, he would have eaten the entire thing in one bite. She was making herself a plate when Ruddy climbed up and laid on top of a towel. She thinks they wore him out. Harrison was trying to get a baseball game on the radio. She curled up in the back of the boat and started to read Kay's novel.

All of a sudden, Harper looked up, and the boat seemed to be drifting. Harrison had his eyes shut, taking a little nap, which is a good thing to do when you're on a boat. Harper woke Harrison up and said, I think we have a problem. This boat is not where it was five minutes ago. Harrison jumped up and went to pull up the anchor, but as he pulled up the rope, it wasn't attached to the anchor.

Harper ventured to say. "Is that a problem?"

"Not really, we will have to go to the marina and have Chuck fix us up with a new one."

All is good with the world. Harrison got a new anchor from the marina.   Harper is not going to let a little thing like losing an anchor ruin her vacation.

She has a beautiful shiny ring on my finger. She can't believe Harrison picked it out; it's perfect. It has one large heart-shaped diamond in the middle then smaller stones on either side. It's Gorgeous. Now we have to talk about the wedding date.

We have only been here for two days, and already she felt very relaxed except for the murder next door. Harper needed to start concentrating on finding the person who killed Howard.

Harper started asking Harrison some questions about the murder. "What all did the officers tell you about this guy. Do they have any suspects? What are we going to do with this dog?"

Let's start at the top. Howard was killed with a baseball bat. That must have hurt. And someone was very mad at him. Why?

After dinner, Harrison was going to take the boat over and get gas.

Harper will take Ruddy for a walk up by the office and ask some questions.

Ruddy and she were walking up to the office. They passed some people from the other cabins. They all wanted to stop and pet Ruddy. He was eating it up. A couple of boys came up to us and asked if that was Mr. Martin's dog.

Harper told them. "Yes, this is Ruddy."

Harper started asking them questions. "Did they know Mr. Martin? Was he a nice man? Did they see or hear anybody fighting with him?" When she got that question out, the boy with the red hair and freckles said. "Do you mean like yelling and screaming?"

The other boy, who had dark hair and wore glasses, said. "There was one guy that came around. He was younger than Mr. Martin, and yelling and screaming was all they did."

"Could you ever understand what they were yelling about?"

Both of the boys shook their heads. "No, they always stayed in the cabin. After a while, the younger guy would get in his car and leave."

"Do you know what kind of car it was?" Harper was crossing her fingers, hoping that the boys might know the make and model of the car.

The red-headed boy said. "It was a blue Ford, an older car, not new and fancy like the ones today." The other boy nodded his head in agreement.

"Okay, boys, Ruddy, and I have to finish our walk. If you think of anything else, please stop by cabin thirteen."

When Harper got to the office, a young girl was behind the counter. Her name tag said, "Molly." Harper started off asking Molly if she heard about Mr. Martin? Molly said, sure everyone has heard about the murder here in the park. Not real good for business. Then Molly turned to the dog and asked, is that Ruddy. Harper informed her it was. Did she know if Mr. Martin had any next of kin? Harper was telling her that the dog showed up on their front porch after all the police cars left. "My fiancé and I are taking care of him. No one has come forward to claim him."

Molly came around the counter and started petting Ruddy, saying what a good dog he was. Ruddy kind of ran all over the park. Mr. Martin was the handyman here at the park. The owners let him stay in cabin fourteen because it needs some work done on the inside, so until they get some extra money to fix it up, Mr. Martin stayed there.

Harper couldn't help herself; she had to ask Molly. "Do you know of anyone that wanted to harm Mr. Martin?"

"Mr. Martin was an old man; I don't think he could ever hurt anyone. Some people didn't care for him; he was slow at fixing things, but he always got the job done eventually. Are you going to keep Ruddy? Molly asked.

"I don't know," Harper had to think about that question.

Molly instructed Harper. "Make sure you keep Ruddy away from Mr. Jeff. Ruddy doesn't like him."

"Who is Mr. Jeff?"

"His full name is Mr. Jeff Henderson; he mows the grass around here. He does odd jobs when the owners need something bigger than what Mr. Martin could do. Just keep Ruddy away from him, okay?"

"Does Mr. Jeff stay here also?"

"No, he has a place in town."

"Thanks, Molly, you have been a big help. Ruddy and I will see you around."

When Harper and Ruddy got back to their cabin Harrison was back, and he was building a fire in the fire pit for later. When it got dark, Harrison and Harper headed for the fire pit. Harper wanted to know if Harrison wanted to make S'more's. He said sure. Harper got out all the Fixin's and headed out to the fire pit. While they were making their S'more's, Harper started telling Harrison all she had learned from Molly. Then Harper posed the question. "What do you think they will do with Ruddy when we leave?" *Harper was thinking maybe if no one claimed him, they could take him home with them.* So, she just came out and asked Harrison. "Can we keep him?"

Harrison's reply was. "As much as I like him, someone will probably claim him in a day or two. Enjoy him for now, but don't set your heart on taking him home."

Harper started smiling. "So, if no one claims him, he could be ours?"

"What did I just say? "Don't set your heart on it." Then as all men do, Harrison asked. "What is on the list for tomorrow?

"I thought maybe we could go into town to that little diner for breakfast if that's okay with you. Then back on the boat. I would like to take a walk around the park just to see what else is here. We could do that before dinner. Dinner is chicken on the grill. Then quiet time by the fire pit."

"Sounds good to me," Harrison smiled.

Harrison put his arm around his new fiancé. "Have I told you lately how much I love you?"

Harper said the same thing back to him.

Chapter Six

Harrison walked in with a cup of coffee for Harper and teased. "Up and at'em, it's Monday already."

"Okay, give me a minute to open my eyes. Oh, you brought me coffee. Thanks."

"It's a beautiful day out there. Would you mind if we try our hand at fishing while we are out on the boat today?"

"No, that sounds like fun. I've never fished before."

They were going to take the boat over, but Harper would have to make lunch, and what would they do with Ruddy?

So, they drove into town for breakfast. During breakfast, Harper asked. "Harrison, did you notice that there was a light on over at Mr. Martin's cabin last night?"

Harrison shook his head. "No, I didn't see any light on. Are you sure it wasn't a reflection from something else?"

"No, there was a light on over there. Who would want to go into that horrible crime scene?"

Harrison recalled the owner telling him he was going to have to get a professional cleaner to come in and clean up that cabin. Maybe it was people there cleaning.

Harper was hoping that was the case and not someone in there messing around.

After breakfast, Harrison found a bait shop to get some worms. Next door to the bait shop was a small general store. Harper went there to pick up some dog food. In the meantime, she had her to-go box with some eggs and hash browns for Ruddy's breakfast. She knew she shouldn't be feeding him, people, food for every meal.

When they pulled up to the cabin, the two boys that Harper had talked to the other day, we're sitting at the picnic table with Ruddy. Harper got out of the car and said. "Hi, what brings you by?"

"You know that guy we told you about the other day? Well, he's here. He's on the baseball field, with some other guys."

Harrison wanted to know what was going on. Harper told him what the boys had said the other day, about this guy who was yelling at Mr. Martin. And Molly up at the office told her his name is Mr. Jeff Henderson. He is a worker around here. Mr. Jeff does the big stuff while Mr. Martin just handled the small projects. Molly also said to keep Ruddy away from this guy; he didn't like him.

"I would like to go and talk to Mr. Jeff before we go out on the boat. I'll only be a minute," Harper said.

Harrison looked at her and remarked. "If you are not back in fifteen minutes, Ruddy and I are going fishing without you."

Harper grabbed the boys and said. "Let's go." They got to the baseball field really fast.

Mr. Jeff was indeed playing baseball. Harper walked over to where he was and asked him to stop for a couple of minutes, she needed a word with him. He did as she asked.

"My name is Harper Gray, and my fiancé and I are staying in cabin thirteen next to Mr. Howard Martins. I was just wondering if you knew anything about his murder."

"Why would I know anything about the old guy getting murdered?"

"Well, I heard you two didn't get along so well. You were always yelling at Mr. Martin even on the day he died."

The two boys were standing behind Harper when Mr. Jeff said. "I suppose those two brats told you that. Those two are a pain in the you know what. They are always causing trouble. Get out of here; I have work to do. Besides, I have already told the police everything I know, so scram. As he lunged forward, the boys took off running. Harper stood there and told Mr. Jeff to knock it off. You have no cause for threatening the boys, or do you?" She turned and left. The boys waited up behind a tree. They all walked back to the cabin. The boys said. "See what we mean. He is a mean man."

Harper thanked the boys for telling her Mr. Jeff was there so she could talk to him. A lot of good that was.

Harrison and Ruddy were both on the boat waiting for Harper. Harrison questioned. "Did you get to talk to Mr. Jeff?

"Oh, yea, he's a piece of work. While we were there, he threatened the boys."

Harrison got up like he was going to get off the boat and talk to Mr. Jeff. Harper calmed him down, and they took off to do some fishing.

Harrison told Harper the best fishing places were up on the other side of the lake. They had not gone that way yet, so Harper was excited to see some more of the lake. This route took them up under a couple of bridges. Harrison took the boat over close to the bank of the lake and got the poles ready. Harrison cast his line while Harper just dropped hers in the water. Harrison was laughing when he told her she should cast her line over by the lake bank because the fish like the muddy water over there. He taught her how to cast. She was getting pretty good at it when all of a sudden, Harper started screaming. Harrison looked at her and blurted out. "What's the matter?"

Harper finally responded. "Something is pulling my line."

"Reel it in," Harrison was telling her. He dropped his line to help her. "Look here; you caught a fish."

"My first fish. Now get it off. That hook is hurting its mouth."

"Okay, okay, give me a minute. This little fish is too small to keep, so we have to let him go."

"Oh, good because I didn't want to eat him."

"You're going to make a great fisherman," Harrison laughed.

They headed over to Turtle Cove for the rest of the time. That is the best spot on this lake. It's quiet; no one comes back here; it's great. But you know what is missing, the turtles. Have you ever see them again?

When they got back to the cabin, the boys were there again. Harper's eyes got really big; what do you think they are doing here again? Harper looked at the boys and remarked, what are you doing here again? They both started talking at the same time. Slow down, guys—one at a time. The red-haired boy talked first. "Mr. Jeff was here snooping around your cabin. Larry and I saw him, so we hid behind a tree to watch him.

Then Larry said. "Yea, he's up to no good. Barry wanted to ask him what he was doing, but not me. I'm not going near the crazy guy. Mr. Jeff also went over to Mr. Martin's cabin and tried to get in, but the doors are locked.

Harrison thanked the boys and told them to stay away from Mr. Jeff.

Chapter Seven

"Harper, you know how I feel about you investigating. But this has gone too far. Could you stay out of this one? Please."

Harper sat there and nodded her head, knowing full well she was not done investigating this murder. She would have to be careful.

Harrison was going to talk to the owner tomorrow about Mr. Jeff.

After dinner, dishes were all done, and Harrison had a fire going in the fire pit. Harper was telling Harrison how excited she was that Liz and Tom would be there day after tomorrow. She was hoping the weather would be beautiful. Tomorrow rain was in the forecast.

Sure enough, when they woke up, it was raining so hard you could hardly see across the street. No boating today.

Harrison inquired. "What are we going to do all day?"

She hugged him and smiled. "Guess."

For breakfast, Harper made bacon, eggs, toast, cheesy grits, and coffee. Harper told Harrison what she had on her list. "Lunch is just sandwiches and dinner; Harper was hoping to go find a nice restaurant. Harper did bring the cribbage board so she could beat him some more. Tomorrow Liz and Tom would be here early, so she was going to make sausage gravy, biscuits, and hash browns. Then lunch on the boat. Dinner was going to be hobo dinners on the gas grill and later peach cobbler with char-coal by the fire pit.

Before they leave Thursday morning, Harper wanted to know. "Can we take them to the diner in town for breakfast? That way, when we get back, I just have to make our lunch and get on the boat for some playtime. We are both getting a good summertime tan. It makes me feel healthy.

Harper finished up the dishes, made the bed, cleaned the bathroom, and checked on the bedroom for Liz and Tom. While she was doing all of that stuff, Harrison was building a fire in the fireplace. It wasn't cold, but a fire made it feel comfortable with all the rain.

Harrison forgot he let Ruddy outside to do his business and forgot to let him back in. He went to the door, and there sat one drowned dog. Before Harrison let Ruddy in, Harrison grabbed a towel to dry him off. Ruddy came in and wanted to shake, but Harrison grabbed him so he wouldn't get water all over the place.

They were both done with the chores. Harper got out the cribbage board and the notebook where she keeps the scores. Harrison got some music on the radio. They sat at the table to play cards. They did that for a few hours. Harper would win a game, then Harrison would win a game.

Harrison begged. "I'm getting hungry. Are you never going to feed me?"

Harper hit him on the arm and told him. "Come and help me get lunch ready."

After lunch, they both kind of laid around being couch potatoes. It was kind of nice doing nothing for a change.

Harrison was taking a nap, so Harper went back to reading Kay's book. She had only given her five chapters, and Harper only read two the other day on the boat. So, she knew she could get through the next three quickly. Kay's book was perfect; of course, this was her seventh in this series. It is a cozy mystery, the kind Harper loves. Someone always dies right off the bat, but you don't know who did it until the very end. That way, you have to keep reading until the end. Kay didn't have a title on this one yet; *I hope she lets me read the rest of the chapters when she gets them done.* So far, a guy gets shot; a blond girl was standing over him with a gun in her hand. But she is not the shooter. Who can it be???

Harrison and Harper headed out for dinner. He told her there was a very nice seafood place just down the road. She wore her sundress she had brought along. Harper felt good with a dress on and the ring on her finger.

When the waiter was taking their order, Harper was telling him about the fish she caught yesterday. Harper ordered the beer-battered fish dinner with hush puppies and coleslaw. Harrison ordered the walleye platter.

Before they left, Harper put some of the dog food in a bowl for Ruddy. He looked at it, not sure if he will eat it or not. We'll see when we get back.

When Harrison opened the door, his mouth dropped, and he started shaking his head. Harper looked around him and saw what had happened. Ruddy sat there wagging his tail, but she thought he knew he was in trouble. Harrison and Harper's slippers were in the front room, partially chewed up. They both had fuzzy slippers with a lot of fuzz in them. Or should we say had a lot of fuzz? It was now all over the front room.

Harper came in and got a hold of Ruddy and was scolding him. She looked over at his bowl of untouched dog food.

"So, this is what you do when we give you dog food. Well, mister, you will not be getting any more people food until you learn to eat what dogs are supposed to eat. DOG FOOD," Harper was trying to be seriously mad at him, but it was so funny, with fuzz all over the place.

Harrison went to get the sweeper. Their slippers were destroyed. He pitched them in the trash. Harrison snickered. "I think this guy needs some toys of his own. Not our slippers."

It's probably our fault since he has no toys. We gave him dog food and left him alone for the first time.

Chapter Eight

Wednesday morning and the sun was shining. Harper got up early to start breakfast. Since Harper wasn't sure if there would be cell service at the cabin, she and Liz talked about what time they were to get there Wednesday morning. Liz said they would be there around nine o'clock.

Harper could get the sausage gravy made and hash browns in a skillet. She wanted to wait to put the biscuits in the oven until right before they got there.

Everything was done; they were just waiting for their guests. Harper had put dog food in Ruddy's bowl and told him, "This is what you get today, so you better eat it up, or you won't be going on the boat with us." Just like he understood, he went over to the bowl and started eating the dog food. "Good Boy," Harper interjected.

All of a sudden, she heard Tom's truck pull up. Harper and Harrison headed out the door. Liz is coming toward Harper, saying LOOK, LOOK holding up her left hand. As Harper is going toward Liz, she had her left hand out, saying LOOK, LOOK. They both stopped and started crying. They grabbed each other's hands to see the rings on each of them. These two were a basket case for a minute. When they stopped and looked at each other's rings, both of them in unison said, "Your ring is beautiful." Harper's was a heart-shaped diamond, and Liz had a solitaire.

Liz grinned. "So, when did Harrison propose? Tom asked me on Saturday night. We went out to dinner, and he asked me while we were at the restaurant." He said. "If he did it in public, maybe I wouldn't say no."

"Harrison proposed Saturday after we had dinner here. Are we not the luckiest girls in the world?" Harper confessed.

In the meantime, Harrison and Tom were congratulating each other. Neither one of them knew the other one was going to propose. The girls went to the kitchen to get the biscuits in the oven. Ruddy was all over everyone. He has never seen so many people before.

Liz bent down and picked up Ruddy. "Who is this precious little thing?"

Harper told her. "This is Ruddy. I don't know if we get to keep him yet or not. He belonged to the man next door, who was murdered. As far as we know, no one has come to claim him yet. He kind of adopted us. I'm afraid I'm getting too attached to Ruddy because if I had to give him up now, it would really hurt."

"You said the man was murdered? Who killed him? Have you figured it out yet?"

"Liz, you are getting as bad as me with three questions in a row. Take a breath. I have a suspect, but of course, Harrison has told me to stay out of it. And you know I will. NOT.... My turn for the questions. How is everything at the store? Have you guys set a date yet? Where are you going to live, your house, or his?"

"Everything at the store is great. The new merchandise with our town's logo on it is a hit. No, we have not set a date yet. What about you guys, have you set a date? About where we are going to live, all four of us will have to build houses next to each other. I can't imagine not living next to you. Tom's house is too big; I know it's where he grew up, and my house is too small, so I think we need to have something of our own."

"Harrison and I haven't even thought about it yet. Or if he has, he hasn't said anything to me. Oh my, I need to start another list." They both laughed.

The timer dinged. "The biscuits are ready. Let's eat; we are wasting sunshine. I can't wait for you to see Turtle Cove."

The girls cleaned up the kitchen, and the guys got the boat uncovered and all the gear onboard. Harper had already made the roll-ups, so they were out the door in no time flat.

"Yes, Ruddy, you get to come also. It's for sure we can't leave you home alone." Harper nodded.

Liz wanted to know what Harper meant about not leaving him home alone.

Harper giggled. "I'll tell you the story when we get on the boat."

The water was so calm today; of course, it was early, not a lot of boats in the water yet. These people liked to sleep late. Harrison and Harper wanted to be the first ones on the water. Because it was still early, there were no boats tied together yet; no one was water skiing, and no, there were no slow fishing boats.

While making their way out to Turtle Cove, Harper started to explain to Liz about Ruddy and why they can't leave him home alone.

"We went out to dinner one night. I had left dog food in Ruddy dish, plenty of water. Well, he decided not to eat the dog food; instead, he found Harrison and my slipper and brought them to the front room. The fuzzy ones, of course. He then proceeded to rip them apart. Fuzz was everywhere. We tried not to laugh at the scene, but it was funny. I tried to scold him, but I was not very convincing about being mad at him. We chalked it up to we left him alone for the first time, and he was mad at us, and he had no toys of his own. So, slippers would have to do."

Liz and Tom were both laughing at this point. "He will surely keep you two on your toes if you get to keep him."

When they reached Turtle Cove, Harper was so excited that her best friend was here with her on a boat at a great place with two wonderful guys.

"This is it. No one comes back this far. They all like to party out on the lake. Give us peace and quiet."

While Harrison was tying off the rafts, he also tossed in some of the noodles.

Ruddy was going crazy, wiggling all over, wagging that tail. Harper kept telling him he had to wait until they were all in the water before he could jump in. He sat down and waited just like he knew what she said.

The water was nice and warm today. They floated on the rafts and played with the noodles in the water most of the day. They only stopped to eat lunch, then back in, they went. Before heading back, Harrison pulled the boat over to land so Ruddy could get out and do his business. All the way back, he laid on Liz's lap and fell asleep. She has a new friend for life.

Everyone got showers; you have to get that lake water and whatever else is in it off your skin.

Harper had everything ready for dinner; the hobo dinners just needed put together. Then on the gas grill, they went. While she and Liz made the salad, the guys started the charcoal for our cobbler out by the fire pit. Ruddy didn't know where to go. He wanted out with the guys, but then he was at the front door and wanted in. In out, in out. Harper stated. "This is the last time, buddy; you stay out with the guys."

Harrison and Tom were tending to the grill while drinking a beer. Liz and Harper had their wine; they were doing just fine.

It was such a nice night. Harper thought they could eat at the picnic table. Liz helped her set the table. They all sat around, waiting for the chicken to get done. Harper had cooked an extra piece of chicken for Ruddy.

Chapter Nine

Tom was surprised how well the chicken turned out by cooking it in foil on the grill. With all the spices added, it turned out rather good. Ruddy loved the chicken. Harper didn't put as many spices on his. *Chicken's good for dogs, right?*

Wait until they taste the peach cobbler with whip cream. The peach cobbler has to cook for almost an hour. Harper didn't want to start it yet. The coals would be ready in about fifteen minutes. They had time to throw the foil away and sit by the fire pit while the guys made them a fire.

Tom said maybe next year they should come up here and rent a cabin and a boat. It is so relaxing. In town, he doesn't get to relax a lot.

Harrison asked him how his business was going. He said he had to hire two more guys; he is getting so busy.

That's when Liz and Harper piped in. "You may need to hire some more guys because since we are all getting married, we will need you to build us houses next door to each other." The guys laughed.

Liz and Harper were serious. We'll talk about this later; they told the guys. Neither one of us couples has even picked out a wedding date yet.

Harrison wanted to know. "You two do not want a double wedding, do you?"

Liz and Harper both said. "No, we each need our own day. Besides, how can we be each other's maid of honor if we were both getting married on the same day? You guys are funny. Men just don't think like us girls do."

Harper said out loud. "I think I would like a winter wedding because then we could go somewhere nice and warm for the honeymoon."

Liz stated. "I think I would like a fall wedding, what do you think about that, Tom?"

He replied. "Baby, whatever your heart desires. The sooner, the better. What if we just take off to Vegas?"

Liz said, rather quickly. "Thomas T Hunter, your mother would kill us. I don't have anyone, so it doesn't matter, but your mother would skin us alive. Besides, I want the whole church thing because I am only getting married once. So, no Vegas for us."

Harrison looked at Harper. "What about Vegas for us. We have no parents, no mothers-in-law who would skin us alive."

Harper also jumped in. "Harrison Lincoln Roberts, you do have a sister that would skin me alive if she could not be at her brother's wedding. We both have friends, and, of course, I want the whole church thing too. So, no Vegas for us either."

Harrison and Tom chimed in. "You women are so easy to please. Church wedding, no Vegas. How easy was that? Tom remarked he wasn't so sure about building houses next to each other." Harrison and Tom both laughed. *They both knew the girls were serious.*

Harrison wanted to know did they have ice cream for the cobbler. Harper told him she only brought a can of whip cream.

"Well, I would like some ice cream. Would you mind if Tom and I walk up to the office to see if they have any?"

"Of course not. It's a peach cobbler, so don't get something strange to go with it," Harper warned.

Not two minutes after the guys left, Mr. Jeff showed up. Ruddy started barking like crazy. Harper had to hold on to him; she thought he would tear Mr. Jeff to pieces.

"What do you want?" Harper declared.

"Just a word of advice. You and your fiancé should get out of here really soon before something else bad happens," Mr. Jeff responded.

Harper was using her outside voice by now. "Are you threatening me? Because if you think I'm afraid of you, you are sadly mistaken. Get out of here before I call the police."

"You may not want to do that until you talk to your little boyfriends." Added Mr. Jeff.

Ruddy was wiggling around so bad and barking that he finally jumped out of Harper's arms and headed toward Mr. Jeff, barking like crazy. Mr. Jeff kept kicking at him when Liz got a hold of Ruddy, and Harper got a hold of Mr. Jeff. Harper yanked his arm and said. "Get out of here."

Just then, Harrison grabbed Mr. Jeff, whipped out his gun, and said. "Make my day, punk." Mr. Jeff took off running.

"Was that Mr. Jeff, the guy you were telling me about?" Tom asked.

"Yes. How did you get back here so fast?" Harper inquired.

"We heard Ruddy barking, so I knew something was wrong."

Harper explained. "He said something about not doing anything until I talked to my little boyfriends. At first, I thought he meant you guys, but now that I think about it, I think he was talking about Larry and Barry. We have to search the park for the boys."

"We should all go up to the office and ask which cabin the boys are in; you are not staying here alone." Harrison proclaimed.

"Okay, let's go."

When they got to the office, Molly was at the front desk. Harper asked her. "Could you tell us which cabin Larry and Barry were staying in?"

Molly looked at her login book and answered. "Thirty and thirty-one, over by the swimming pool."

The four of them headed to the pool when they found thirty and thirty-one. They knocked on cabin door thirty, and a red-headed gentleman, Barry's dad, came to the door. Harper asked for Barry, but his dad said he and his cousin Larry were out and about.

Harrison started telling Barry's dad about Mr. Jeff.

Harper inquired. "Does Larry live over in thirty-one?"

"Yea, that's my wife's brother. Let me get him; then we can find the boys. Then this, Mr. Jeff. By the way, I'm Ted, and my brother-in-law is Wayne."

"Oh, by the way, I'm Harrison and my fiancé Harper and our friends Liz and Tom."

They went over to the pool area, but the boys were not there. They tried the tennis courts and volleyball courts, no boys. Where could they be? Ted suggested we split up and meet back at the pool in thirty minutes. Ted and Wayne headed one way, and the four of us headed the other. When they found them, they were clear over by the boat ramp. They headed back over to the pool area where their dads were waiting.

Harper started off wanting to know something about Mr. Jeff that no one else knows? Mr. Jeff said. "That my fiancé and I should get out of here real soon before something else bad happens around here. Do you boys have any idea what he meant by that?"

The boys shook their heads and said. "Not a clue, the guy is crazy. We think he is the one that killed Mr. Martin."

Harrison started questioning the boys now. "What makes you say that? Did you see him around the day Mr. Martin was found?"

"No, not him, but that blue car was out in front of Mr. Martin's cabin, and we are pretty sure it belongs to Mr. Jeff. We could hear yelling, and Ruddy was barking up a storm. We high tailed it out of there to go tell our parents what was going on, but when we got back, the car and the guy were gone."

Chapter Ten

Harrison expressed growing concern. "What do you think he meant by get out of here real soon before something else bad happens around here?"

On their way back to the cabin, they stopped and picked up some ice cream for the cobbler. Harper was praying the peach cobbler had not burned. Everything was fine when they returned except there was a blue car in Mr. Martin's driveway, but there was no one in sight. Wait; there is a light on in Mr. Martin's cabin. Harrison went over and knocked on the door. A tall man answered. "Yea, what do you want?"

"My name is Harrison Roberts. My fiancé and I are renting the cabin next door to Mr. Martin. What are you doing in his cabin?"

The guy replied, rather smartly. "Well, my name is Roger, and what business is it of yours if I'm here or not?"

"The guy that used to live here was murdered. Are you the murderer returning to the scene of the crime?"

"Do I look like a murderer?"

"Yes, you do."

"Howard was my brother; I came by to see if I needed to clean anything out of here."

Harper spoke up. "Your car was here last Saturday, and the neighbors heard yelling. What were you arguing with your brother about?"

"My brother and I always argued. He was a slob, a no-good bum."

"Is there anyone you can think of that wanted him dead?"

"I'm sure there were lots of folks who could have killed him. Me being one of them, but I didn't kill him."

While Harrison and Harper talked to Roger, Tom and Liz went up to the front office to get the owner and have him come and get rid of this guy.

When the owner Johnny Jones came back with Tom and Liz, he went straight over to the cabin and told Roger to clear out but first give him the keys to the cabin.

He yelled at Roger. "I never want to see you again on my property. Do you understand, Roger?"

Roger was throwing a fit, going on and on about. "All my brother's things are all here. They're mine now." Johnny told him. "You have ten minutes to grab whatever belongings of Howard's you want and get out."

Roger stomped around but never grabbed anything. Out the front door, he went after he threw the keys to Johnny.

Johnny was so glad Roger was gone. Harper had to ask. "What is with him?"

"He is a big pig. He and Howard never got along. I think because Howard had a job and people who would look out for him. Roger was a big bully. Always yelling at Howard, never saying a nice word to him or anyone. I wouldn't put it past Roger for killing Howard."

"Johnny, can you tell us about Mr. Jeff?" Harper asked.

"Sure, Mr. Jeff is one of our employees; he mows the grass and does bigger repairs around here when Howard couldn't."

"Was there any love lost between Howard and Mr. Jeff?"

"Not that I know of; they seemed to get along just fine."

"Okay, thanks for all your help."

After everyone left, the four of them sat around eating the peach cobbler with ice cream and pondered what was said about each man. Liz and Tom thought Roger was the killer. Because he had motive and opportunity, he was here that Saturday, and he despised his brother.

On the other hand, Harper and Harrison believed the killer was Mr. Jeff. The owner didn't know about the animosity between him and Howard. Mr. Jeff seemed like the bully around here. Harper still didn't understand why they should leave before something else bad happens around here.

Harper's brain was tired; she wanted to go to bed and get some rest. They all said their goodnights.

Thursday morning was here before they knew it. They were going to drive over to the little diner that had the big meals. Then Liz and Tom had to head home.

After their orders arrived, Liz and Tom could not believe how big the portions were.

While they ate, Liz told Harper. "I think we have a budding romance starting in town."

"OH, we do? Who would that be?"

"Your Kay and Nick James over at the Good Time Bar. *Nick owns the Good Time Bar over on Main and Maple Street. He has been there for years, never married. A confirmed bachelor. Nick is one of the last of the good guys.* I've seen them over in the square and over at Rosie's Diner." (Rosie's Diner is on the other side of Main Street. Rosie owns and runs the place. She is rather short and stocky with large hands, and she always smells like grease. It is a gathering place for people to come and gossip, eat greasy food, and have a good time.)

"We have only been gone for four days. When did this all start?"

"I don't know, but you'll have to ask Kay when you get home."

"You better believe I will."

After breakfast, they hugged and said their goodbyes. "We'll see you guys on Saturday. Travel safe."

Harrison and Harper headed back to the cabin and packed up some roll-ups for lunch, and headed to the boat. Harper remembered to take Kay's chapters to finish reading. Last time Harper started reading, she nodded off for a few minutes. She was bound and determined to finish them today. Ruddy was waiting by the front door; he knew something was up. In his little brain, all he heard was boat ride, boat ride. He's such a silly dog. Harper hoped they could keep him. She had better talk this over with Harrison today.

They finally made it to the boat. Harper said she doesn't know what she loves more the lake or Harrison. Oh, of course, Harrison, on the lake.

Chapter Eleven

When they arrived at Turtle Cove, guess what? There sat two turtles on a stump out in the water. Harper was taking so many pictures; it was unreal.

Ruddy saw them too, but Harper told him to stay away from them; they are probably snapping turtles, and they will get you. Ruddy sat there with his head turned sideways thinking. *Are you sure?*

Harrison had tied the rafts off, so in the water, they all went.

Again, Harper told Ruddy to stay away from the turtles.

The turtles stayed sunning themselves for a while, then they climbed off the stump and swam away.

Harper started asking Harrison. "What do you think about keeping Ruddy? No one has come to claim him, and I don't think Roger wanted him. You know I cannot just leave him here to fend for himself."

Harrison suggested. "I should call the police department and ask them. If they say it's okay, then we will take him home with us." Harper came over and hugged Harrison so tight, telling him; she loved him so much.

Harper thought her life was perfect. She had a man who loved her and maybe a dog that was house broke. Now she just had to convince Tom and Harrison that she and Liz needed homes built beside each other.

Harper turned the conversation to their wedding date. "Would a winter wedding be okay with you, or do you think it's too soon?"

Harrison looked at Harper and said. "Tomorrow wouldn't be too soon. Whenever you want the wedding, it's okay with me."

"Fine, maybe we should look at the first part of December. I don't want to get married to close to Christmas. Then we can honeymoon someplace warm. Like Aruba."

"Baby, you tell me when and where to show up, and I will be there."

"But I want your input. Remember, you always say it's the journey, not the destination. Planning it all is half the fun. You have to help me with the journey, the planning. Is it a deal?"

"Deal." Here they are out in the middle of Turtle Cove kissing and hugging what a sight. "Are you ready to head back in?"

"Sure, dinner tonight is flatbread pizzas. Tomorrow is a leftover day."

"Flatbread pizza sounds great. Have I thanked you for all your hard work you have put into this vacation? The meals have been wonderful. If you had left it up to me, we would have had peanut butter and jelly for every meal. You thought of everything. I think Tom was impressed with the hobo dinners. I know I was. Thank you, babe," as he gave her a big kiss.

Harper was getting concerned that she has not broken the case yet. She only had one more day. Maybe she needs to set a trap. Boy, she wishes her sleuthing buddy Aggie was here to help her. (Aggie was Harper's neighbor who lives across the street. She has assisted in Harper's sleuthing projects before. Harper isn't sure if

Aggie is or was with the CIA. Aggie never reveals too much about her past.)

Harrison was starting the boat when big black smoke came pouring out of the back of the boat.

Harrison looked at it and said. "Well, that's not good."

Harper wanted to know. "Are we stranded out here?"

Harrison had a strange look on his face. "For now, we are."

"What are we going to do?"

"Give me a minute to check on the outboard motor. Don't panic just yet."

"Okay, we are officially stranded. Harper see if your cell phone has any towers. If you can, call the marina."

Harper's phone had towers, and she dialed the marina. The owner, Chuck, answered now Harper is talking a mile a minute. "This is Harper Gray and Harrison Roberts. He rented a pontoon boat for the week. We are stranded back here in Turtle Cove. The outboard motor blew up. Can you help us?"

Chuck wasn't sure where Turtle Cove was. Harrison took Harper's phone and told Chuck. "We're out at the cove."

Chuck said. "Oh, I know where you are. I just never heard anyone call it Turtle Cove."

"When my parents used to bring my sister and me out here during the summer, we would end up back in the cove. One day when we pulled in, two turtles were sitting on a stump out in the water, so my sister and I named the place Turtle Cove."

"I like that, good story. Sit tight. I'm on my way out to Turtle Cove."

Harrison told Harper that the owner Chuck was on his way to get them so that they will be out of here in no time.

When Chuck arrived, he tied up the pontoon boat to his skiff. "I'll have you back in no time. How many more days do you have on the rental?"

"Tomorrow is our last full day. Saturday morning, we will be leaving bring the boat back over from the campground."

"You're in luck. I have one pontoon boat left. You can have that one. We'll fix you right up when we get back to the marina."

After they transferred all their things from one boat to the new boat, Chuck was correct; he fixed them up lickety-split. They were in the new boat and headed for their cabin.

When they pulled into their dock, they saw someone running away from their campsite. Someone had turned the picnic table up-side-down. And the ashes from the fire pit were scattered everywhere. Harrison tried to chase the person who was running but lost him. Harper said she and Ruddy would go to the office and get Johnny.

Johnny came back with Harper and Ruddy on his golf cart. Everyone here seemed to have a cart of some kind.

Harper was getting ready to go in the cabin when Harrison told her to wait; he wanted to go in with her just in case someone was in there messing around. The coast was clear. No one was in the cabin. Ruddy searched the cabin room by room, sniffing everything. You would have thought he was a bloodhound, not just a mutt.

Johnny asked Harrison. "Did you get a good look at the person you saw running away?"

Harrison said. "No, the guy headed into the woods, and that is where I lost him."

Chapter Twelve

Harper was wondering. *Why would someone want to mess with us? We haven't done anything to anyone.*

Harper was thinking everything was going so good until all the crazy stuff started happening. She started a list, now she is reading it to Harrison.

- *Saturday - The first day someone was found murdered in the cabin beside them.*
- *Sunday - The second day out on the boat lost the anchor.*
- *Monday – Ruddy chewed up slippers.*
- *Tuesday – It rained most of the day.*
- *Wednesday – Liz, and Tom here. Good thing.*
- *Thursday – Outboard motor blew up. Back at the cabin, someone turned their picnic table over and spread the ashes from the fire pit everywhere.*

"Is this what Mr. Jeff meant by get out before something bad happens."

Harrison said. "It's just a coincidence that all of these things were happening. Harper, you are reading too much into what Mr. Jeff said. None of these things were life-threatening. Do you think Mr. Jeff could have made the anchor fall off, or the motor blows up? And you know he made Ruddy tear up our slippers. Think about it, Harper, it's just stuff that happened. When Mr. Jeff said that you put it in your subconscious mind, and now you believe it all relates to Mr. Jeff."

"You're right; I do get carried away sometimes. I know I don't like Mr. Jeff, but we are going to think happy thoughts about Friday, our last day here."

"Harrison, are you ready for dinner? We're having flatbread pizza."

"Sure, that sounds good along with a cold beer, that'll hit the spot."

Harper told Harrison he had to help her. He had to put the topping on his pizza that he wanted. She had pepperoni, some ham from the roll-ups, a jar of mushroom, and some green peppers leftover from the salad.

"Put whatever you want on it, then we will put them in the oven. No grilling tonight." Harrison loaded his with everything. Harper only put pepperoni on hers, along with the sauce and the cheese.

Harrison asked. "How long before the pizza is ready?"

"It shouldn't take long. Maybe fifteen to twenty minutes."

He said. "I probably had time to call the police chief and see what they have to say about Ruddy."

Harper could hardly contain herself. She sat next to him while he talked to the chief. Harrison kept saying. "Oh, I see, Oh, alright."

Harper couldn't stand it another minute. She was grabbing his arm going. "Well, what did he say?"

Harrison hung the phone up, and with a big smile on his face, he said. "Looks like Ruddy will become Ruddy Roberts. Mr. Martin only had one brother, and he didn't want Ruddy. No one else has inquired about him, so the chief said that if we wished to take him, we could otherwise, the chief would have to take him down to the dog pound. And you know what they will do to him there."

Harper called for Ruddy; he came running she picked him up and asked him if he wanted to become Ruddy Roberts. You're going to go home with us on Saturday. Of course, he knew what she was saying, and he started barking. Good Dog.

Friday was a sad day. It was the end of a wonderful vacation. Harper hated to leave the cabin and the lake. They will be back maybe next year, along with Liz and Tom.

Harper was fixing breakfast from leftovers. Harper found eggs, bacon, ham, green peppers, and cheese. She decided to make them each an omelet. Lunch was whatever she could find. Dinner was going to be burgers on the gas grill, and mac and cheese in the crock-pot.

Harper started the mac and cheese before they headed out on the boat. Turtle Cove was the best. The sun was shining, and all was right with the world. The anchor was there; the motor didn't blow up; there were

no more dead people laying around. It was all good.
Harper even finished Kay's five chapters of her new
book. Now she can't wait to read the rest of the story.

Harper couldn't wait to get back home to show off
her engagement ring. She was on cloud nine. Now they
just had to set a date and get Tom to build the two houses
next to each other. She was feeling kind of sad because
she never figured out who killed poor Mr. Martin. Oh,
well, you can't win them all.

While they were on the boat, Ruddy was a riot. He
was on the deck of the boat and jumped as far out as he
could. Then he would head back and want on the boat
again. Harrison played this game with him for a little
while. One-time, Harrison told Ruddy to climb up on the
back of the boat and jump off. That is what Harrison and
his sister Hannah used to do. When Ruddy got up on the
back of the boat, he stood there for a minute, like look at
me. I'm the king of the mountain, and he wagged his tail
and jumped. Oh, what a sight. Ruddy and Harrison were
getting tired of this game, so they both got on a raft and
just floated around.

Harper thought my two boys had worn themselves out. They will sleep good tonight.

As they pulled into the dock for the last time, it was bittersweet. Next year is all Harper kept saying. It wasn't time for dinner yet, so Harrison and Harper started clearing out the boat. They got all the towels, the cooler, they let the air out of the rafts. When Harrison takes the boat back over to the marina, he will fill the gas tank then.

Harper had taken her shower first so she could start dinner. It was just burgers and mac and cheese. The mac and cheese Harper had put in the crock-pot before they left. She had it on low, so it was just fine. She made the hamburger patties, so when Harrison finished with his shower, he could start the grill. After dinner, they made one last fire in the fire pit. They sat out by the fire for quite some time. There will be other vacations and more time spent here on Shadow Lake. The end of vacations are always mixed with emotions!

Chapter Thirteen

It was Saturday and time for them to leave, but they were going home with more than they had come with…..Ruddy was headed home with them. Harper couldn't be happier.

Harper had to make a list again. She made it once, but she didn't write it down because she wasn't sure she was going to get to keep him, but now she knows for sure, so here goes the list:

- Call Vet on Monday.

- Get more dog food.

- Get Ruddy a license.

- Get him toys.

- Get him a bed.

- Get him two bowls, one for water one for food.

- Get him a leash.

Harper will think of a thousand other things he will need later.

Ruddy was a great traveler. He loved the boat, and he was perfect in the car on the ride home. Ruddy had laid on the back seat and was snoozing. Some dogs get hyper when they travel. When they pulled into the drive, his head popped up. Harper let him out but told him. "Don't run off cause I'm not going to chase you all over the place. Ruddy, this is where you are going to live from now on. I'll show you around later. For now, we have to get the car unpacked."

When Ruddy got out, he started sniffing everywhere. Harper laughed at him. Guess he was checking for other dogs in his yard. Ruddy was so good he never left the yard. He followed Harrison and her in and out while unpacking. He never really went into the house, yet he would wait for them to come back out to get more stuff out of the car.

When Harrison finished, he said. "Come on, boy; let's go check out your new home."

Harrison opened the door, and Ruddy walked right in, Harper said. "Welcome home, Ruddy." He took off sniffing everything in the house. He finally was done checking out the house when the back door opened, and someone said. "Yoo-hoo, it's me." It was Liz. She and Harper come and go to each other's house by way of the back door.

They always say, "Yoo-hoo." Of course, Ruddy came flying into the kitchen barking until he saw that it was Liz. He remembers her from up at the lake, smart dog. Liz bent down and patted Ruddy's head while saying. "Hi, there, new neighbor." Liz looked at Harper and said. "I see you got your way."

Harper said. "Stop that! Harrison loves this little guy as much as I do. I think it might be the other way around. Harrison got his way." They both laughed.

Harrison talked to the police chief up at the lake and said no one has inquired about him, so if we didn't take him, the chief would have to take him to the pound. Well, you know we weren't going to let that happen. So here he is, our new live-in pet.

Liz mentioned how nice it would be to have a pet in the neighborhood. Just so, he does his business in your yard, not mine. She laughed.

Liz proceeded to ask Harper since they just got home, would they like to come over for dinner. "That way Harper, you don't have to go grocery shopping right away or think about dinner. You can always go out for breakfast and do your shopping later."

Harper said. "That sounded like a plan. What time should we come over?" Of course, then Harper said. "What do you want me to bring." Harper put her hand on her forehead and said. "I'm sorry, how about if I just bring a cute guy."

Liz said. "That would work."

They scheduled dinner at six o'clock. That gave Harrison time to go home and put some of his stuff away. "While I'm out, do you need me to stop and get anything?" Harrison asked Harper.

"No, I think we are okay until we do some shopping tomorrow. I have coffee, and I still have a couple of cans of dog food. We may have to go out for breakfast because I still feel like we are on vacation."

Harrison said. "I am on vacation until Monday afternoon."

Harper started a load of wash after Harrison had left. She was sitting at the kitchen table, making a shopping list. Then Harper wondered if Ruddy would like some dry dog food. Maybe she would ask the vet on Monday, which kind was better for Ruddy.

Harrison was back in no time. He sat at the table with Harper and grabbed her hand, and said. "We need to talk."

Harper got nervous. "Why, babe, what's going on?"

Harrison proceeded to tell her that two houses weren't working out for him any longer. Maybe she should move in with him, or he could move in with her.

She got a big smile on her face and said. "You moving in with me makes more sense. My back yard is fenced in for Ruddy, and of course, Liz lives next door. One of these days, we will have a new house that is both of ours. But until Tom builds them, we are stuck living here." She laughed.

"You are serious about the two houses being built side by side so you and Liz will not be apart?"

"Yep. We are best friends. I have never known anyone like Liz; we never argue. She understands me when I need a little nudge or a shoulder to cry on. I know you guys don't get it, but we are serious."

"Tonight, at dinner, we need to talk to Tom about finding us some land to building two houses. He is so good at what he does. Now we have to figure out what kind of home do we want? A ranch, a two-story, a castle or a cave. I have a ranch, and you have a two-story, which one do you like better?" Harper asked.

Harrison had to say. "I preferred the ranch style. I like everything on one floor. Since we get to design it, our master suite could be on one side of the house and a couple of bedrooms on the other of the house. What do you think?"

Harper stated she loved her ranch. "Growing up, we lived in a two-story, and I hated the stairs. And when we are old and gray, we may not be able to do steps. So, a ranch it is, with a large fenced in yard for Ruddy and all the kids we are going to have."

"Whoa, we need to discuss how many kids we want."

Chapter Fourteen

Harper went on to say they had plenty of time to decide on how many kids they wanted. First, we have to get Tom to build the houses.

Harrison then declared he would be moving in with Harper. He knew better than to have her move away from her friend Liz. He was happy that Harper had such a good and loyal friend. They're hard to come by. He would be giving up his hot tub, but he can always put a new one on the deck of their new home.

Harper fed Ruddy; then, they headed over to Liz's house. With a "Yoo-hoo, it's us." they went in the back door. Something was smelling good. Harper asked Liz. "Can I help with anything?"

"Of course, Liz said. "I have it handled."

They had stuffed pork chops with cheesy potatoes, brown sugar carrots, and applesauce.

What a wonderful meal they all shared.

Harper told them that she and Harrison had talked about who would put their house up for sale first. We decided Harrison should put his up first.

"Now Tom, when can you start finding us some land to build our homes on?" Harper wanted to know.

Tom turned his head and stared at Harper. "You and Liz are serious about this."

Liz replied. "You bet we are. Isn't there a new development over at Robbins Acres, or are they only building condos?"

Tom was doing some work over there, and they are just condos. But down the road at Pinnacle Acres, the last time Tom drove by, *which was yesterday,* they have some beautiful large parcels of land you build your own house on.

"Are you kidding me? You drove over there and didn't tell me." Liz was looking right at Tom shaking her head.

"Well, I can't tell you everything if I wanted it to be a surprise."

"Do you mean we can buy the land, and you will build our two houses?" Harper and Liz were asking.

"You bet I will, but first, Harper and Harrison have to see the place they may not like it."

"When can we go see the land?" Harper questioned.

"How about right now?"

"Okay, let's go."

On the way over to Pinnacle Acres, the girls couldn't stop talking. They were so excited.

When they got there, the development was huge. There was so much land. How do we know which lot is which? Tom said, look on the sign; it tells how big the lot. On one side of the road, there were trees in the back yard on the other side. There weren't any.

Harper asked Harrison, do you want trees or no trees. He wanted trees, and so did Liz.

"Okay, Tom show us some large lots with trees and your lot right next door. Remember, I don't want to be at the corner of any street."

They looked at all the signs and finally found two that were identical. Somewhat in the back of the development. Harper said she likes the lots here in the back.

Harrison said they would have to talk to the developer and find out how much each property cost. Tom thought they started at around thirty thousand. Then you have to build your house. Liz wanted to make sure Tom could be the builder. He said, of course, but he will need a second crew. He can't finish their house and wait to build Harpers. He could see it now; they work on Liz's house one day, and the next day they work on Harper's. This will be a riot.

Tom wanted to know if they were looking for a ranch or a two-story. Harrison told him that he and Harper had talked about it, and they wanted a ranch. With a big deck on the back and a big porch on the front. Harrison wanted to know how will they get plans for each house.

Tom reassured Harrison he had a million plans. We should stop by his office and look at some. Liz has already picked out the house she wants, and it's a ranch also.

Tom said. "I hope they don't pick out the same one. Wouldn't that be funny."

Harrison asked. "Could Harper and I stop by his office on Monday to look at house plans."

Harrison said. "The sooner, the better because I know how Harper is going to bug me to death until we pick out our home."

Tom went on to tell Harrison. "Why don't we stopover at the office on the way back to Liz's. I have a million house planning books you can take some with you, and Harper can start looking right away. That way, Liz can show her what house she picked out."

"That sounds like a plan. Harper will be thrilled," Harrison commented.

Tom was driving all of them back to Liz's when he turned off and headed for his office. Harper got a funny look on her face, then asked. "Are we going right now to pick out a plan for our home?"

Tom said. "No, we are going to the office to pick up some house planning books for you to take home and start looking for your home. Liz can show you the house we picked out so you can't have it. The developer doesn't want all the homes to look alike, so you have to pick out your own."

Liz started telling Harper. "The one we picked out is a three-bedroom ranch. The front door is on the side of the house. The front porch isn't very big, but we made up for it with the extra-large deck on the back. It has a two-car garage. It has a full basement. The laundry room is on the first floor along with the master suite and two-bedrooms or one-bedroom and an office for Tom. We can always add more bedrooms in the basement if we need to. Wait until you see it, I love it. Did I tell you the front-room has a gas fireplace and a cathedral ceiling, and it is open to the dinning-room and the kitchen is in the front of the house? All of it is open. I can't wait for you to see it for yourself."

Chapter Fifteen

Harper couldn't wait either. When they got to Tom's office, Liz went straight over and grabbed a big book; she turned right to the page she wanted, her and Tom's Home. So, their house was long, and it had an open concept. The kitchen was in the front of the house, then the foyer, the dining room, and the living room with large windows and a fireplace. A door off the living room was out to the back deck; it even had enough room for a hot tub and a large grill. Off the kitchen was a door to the two-car garage. When you walk into the foyer, there was another door that led to the full basement. Next to that was a long hallway first door to the left was a closet. To the right was another coat closet, and that led into the master suite. It had a large walk-in closet and their bath-room. The next door on your way down the hallway was a bathroom on the right on the left was the laundry room. At the end of the hall were two bedrooms.

Liz started pulling out books for Harper to check out. Some of them had nothing but ranch-style homes, and some had two-story homes. Harper, like Liz, was only interested in the ranch homes.

Tom told Harper to take a couple home, so she and Harrison can look through them. There was no hurry; they weren't going to start building tomorrow even though the girls would have liked that to happen.

Harper gave Harrison one of the books she brought home, and she took the other one. She was describing what all she wanted in a home,

two to three bedrooms, a master suite, a large kitchen loaded with all the latest cooking equipment. A laundry room on the first floor.

Harrison was telling Harper what he was looking for in a home, which was just about everything that Harper wanted. He did mention he would like a full basement, a two-car garage, a big back deck for the hot tub. While Harrison was looking in one of the books, he looked up and asked Harper. "What about a swimming pool? Would you like that? Can we afford one?"

Harper started telling Harrison. "I've told you before that money is not a problem. My parents left me plenty, and then when Jack died, I don't even know how much his estate was worth. *Jack was the owner of the building with the four apartments and the drug store below. He was also Harper's older half-brother that she didn't know about. Her mother was very young when she had him, and she couldn't raise a baby all by herself. When Harper moved to Addison, Jack knew right away who she was, but he didn't tell her. He said he was afraid she would hate him. So, until the lawyer read the will to Harper, she had no idea. They had become good friends. He left his entire estate to her.*

And then there was Helen's estate. *Helen was the eighty-seven-year-old lady that rented one of Jack's apartments. Well, one night, she went to take a bath and had a massive heart attack while in the tub with the water running. Nate, one of the employees from the drug store, lived in Jack's old apartment. He heard the water running for a long time, so he went over to investigate. The poor lady was already dead. Her estate was to go to Jack, but Jack died first, and Helen never changed her*

Helen didn't have very much money, but what was there, Harper was giving it to the Garden Club Girls. They can use it for all kinds of things.

Harper told Harrison. "Baby, don't worry about money."

"Harper, I have a good job, and good pay, I'm not a gigolo."

"That's not what I meant, and you know it."

When they got home, Harper couldn't put the book down when all of a sudden, Harper shouted. "This is the one, Harrison, look at it. It's perfect." She started telling him all about it. You go in the front door turn to the right; that's the master suite off of it is a large closet with built-in dressers. A large bathroom with a room just for the toilet. The shower you could hold a convention in it there were two shower heads, one on one end of the shower and another on the opposite wall rain showers above each end. There was a whirlpool tub and double sinks. The bathroom was almost as big as the bedroom. When you come out of the bedroom on the right was the basement door. Straight ahead was a formal living-room. Turn to the right, and there is the dinning-room, sliding glass doors leading out to the deck right again is the large kitchen. To the left of the dinning-room was a large family room with a fireplace. The kitchen, dining room, and den were all open concept. At the other end of the family room to the left, there were two bedrooms and one bathroom. Off the family room was a smaller room, which was the laundry room with a half bath. A side door out to the two-car garage. Harrison said he liked it a lot, but maybe they should keep looking. Harper said. "Sure, but I'm already living in this house. Plus, its name is "The Clover House," and you know how I am about clovers." Harper can just be walking down the street and look down, and she can find a four-leaf clover. She has a book with all the states she has been too, and a four-clover from each of those states.

Harper will have to ask Liz if her house has a name. They finally headed to bed, where Harper was going to dream about "The Clover House."

Sunday morning was here before they knew it, and they were both starving but had no food in the house. They headed over to have brunch at the Village Restaurant. When they walked in, they spotted Liz and Tom, and Harper asked them if they could join them; of course, they said sure. Now Harper could ask Liz if her house had a name. She said its name was "The Princess House," and Tom said he thought that should be their house.

Harper told Liz she was pretty sure she found their house, but Harrison wanted to keep looking. Our home is "The Clover House." Liz said. "How appropriate." Harper has this thing about finding four-leaf clovers.

Tom and Harrison were talking about going to see the developer tomorrow and find out about the land. He told Tom. "I'm pretty sure Harper has picked out our house. She saw it in the book, and now she claims she is living in it. Women, what are we going to do with them?"

When Harper and Harrison got home, Ruddy had not chewed on anything. Good dog, and he ate his dog food. Harper let him out back for a while. The yard was fenced in so he couldn't runoff. They would have to be careful where they stepped when they went back there. Harper knew it would be her job to clean up after Ruddy, but that was okay; she loved him so much she could handle cleaning up the pooh.

Harper sat at the kitchen table and started making a shopping list. With no food in the house, she would need a list; otherwise, she would go crazy and buy everything.

Harrison said. "After the grocery store, maybe we should go over to my place and start bringing some of my things over here," Harper agreed.

Harper questioned Harrison about the land and how soon does he think Tom can start to build?

Harrison told her to stay calm; they were going to talk to the developer tomorrow. Then once we have the land, he was sure Tom would start on the houses.

Chapter Sixteen

Harrison was gathering up some of his clothes. He already had some of his shaving things over at Harper's. Harper suggested they take a break and discuss what, if any, of the big pieces of furniture they wanted to keep.

Harrison told her whatever she didn't want; she would not hurt his feelings if it had to go to the dump. Harper had some excellent points. They needed to keep his couch for the new family room, and hers could go in the formal living room. She had a front room now but never used it, so the furniture was brand new. Harper didn't have a dining room, only the kitchen table, so they should keep Harrison's dining room set. It had six chairs, the table, and a buffet. They would take all of that when Harper asked Harrison about the china closet. He said he would love to find a place for it; it was his mothers. Of course, Harper agreed. Now, who's bedroom set would they keep. Harper's was newer, but they did have two extra bedrooms, so maybe they would take all the sets from Harrison's. He reminded Harper that they didn't need two bedrooms right off the bat so, possibly one room could be his workout room? And when the time comes, the other room will be a nursery. Let's not take all the bedroom sets. She thought about it, and he was right; they didn't need all those beds just yet. They discussed leaving all the appliances. The houses would probably sell better if they left them. I mean, they were building a brand-new house so they would get to pick out all the new appliances.

Harrison questioned. "Do I get to keep my man-size recliner?"

"Well, of course, you do. How could I take that away from you? You need someplace to put your feet up after a long day on the job."

Harrison has started this new thing; he puts his hand backward on his forehead and says, "Don't worry about me."

"Don't worry about me," he stated.

Harper walked over to him and hit him in the arm. He thinks he is so funny sometimes.

They started talking about all the kitchen stuff. Harper already had most every new thing that came out. She has an instant pot, crock-pots, mixer, toaster, coffee pot, pots, and pans, dishes. You name it, and she has it. Maybe we should have a garage sale to get rid of some of this stuff. All the things we need to keep, we will probably need a storage unit to put all the furniture in until our house is built. Harper doesn't have room at her place to store it.

When they got back to Harper's, they had lots of stuff to carry in. Harper said they should put it all in the spare bedroom for now and go through it later when she had made some room in the closet for Harrison's clothes. She will need to get one of his dressers over here for his things. After all of that, they were done for the day. Harper asked Harrison if he was hungry yet; he shook his head. He overate at the brunch, so food didn't even sound appealing right now.

Liz came over and did her usually "Yoo-hoo" and walked in the back door. "What are you guys doing? I saw you carrying a lot of stuff from Harrison's into your house Harper. Oh, wait, are you moving in Harrison?"

"That I am. I have been dating this woman for a while, and since we are engaged, we thought it was time. What about you and Tom. When are you two going to move in together?"

"We did talk about it, but he has so much stuff it would never fit into my little house, and I'm not moving into his big old place. We've decided to wait until the new house is built. Tom seems to think once you guys talk to the developer, tomorrow he will be able to start building right away. Before the snowfalls. Won't that be great? He also said he is going to hire a few more guys to start on your house too. So, they should both be done at the same time. Have you guys picked out a wedding date yet?"

Harper answered that question. "Yes, we have. It's going to be Saturday, December 1st, 2018. Then off to Aruba for a honeymoon. What about you guys, what date did you pick?"

Liz stated. "Saturday, October 20 th, 2018

"WOW, we better get started figuring things out. You have less time than we do. Do you think the houses will be built by then?"

"This is only the end of June, so we still have July, August, September, and part of October. Tom thinks he can have both houses built in around three months. He said as long as we can decide what we want in a timely manner, and neither one of us changes anything on the blueprints. You do realize, Harper. We have to pick out everything, the doors, doorknobs, kitchen cabinets, sink, stove, refrigerator, paint color, hardwood, or carpet. What kind of bathtub do you want? There are a million things to pick out."

Harper agreed there were a lot of things that needed to be decided on to building a house. Harper told Harrison, you and Tom better get started with the developer tomorrow.

All Harper could think of was all the lists she was going to have to make. List about the house, list about the wedding, who knows what else.

It's Monday morning, and the four of them met over at Rosie's Diner. Rosie's was just that, a diner. Greasy food and a gossip joint. Rosie, who owned it, was a character. Rosie's was on Main Street just down from the Village Restaurant, where Harper works as a server. Aaron Archer owns The Village Restaurant. It serves higher-end food. They are only open for lunch and dinner.

Across the street from the Village Restaurant is the Main Street Drug Store, where Liz works.

They ordered coffee; then, the guys headed over to the development, and the girls headed over to the drug store. Harrison and Tom came into the store an hour later and headed to the office to talk to Liz and Harper. They didn't look pleased.

Chapter Seventeen

Liz and Harper jumped up and ran to the guys and said. "You two, don't look very happy. What's going on?" Harper asked.

Harrison said. "I think you two better sit down. Our news is not good. The developer was thrilled that we wanted to build two houses on the lots right now, but the problem is, there are no lines put in yet like the water, sewer, gas, electric. He is hoping they are all in before winter, but he can't guarantee anything. So, either we find another development, or we wait until spring to start our builds.

He said if we could hold off, he would give us a break on the price of the lots."

Tom added. "I know you girls wanted your houses built as soon as possible but, there are no other suitable developments right now. So, unless we bought land and put all the utilities on it ourselves, we have to wait, I'm afraid."

Harper wanted to know how much the utilities would cost?

Tom told her a lot, times two. It really would be better if we waited.

The girls were disappointed, but they understood. They did love the lots they picked out. And that is where they wanted their houses.

They looked at each other and said, well, we now have more time to concentrate on our weddings. And selling at least one of our houses, and picking out more stuff for our homes. The guys just sat there, shaking their heads. "Oh, what have we done?"

Harrison wanted to know if anyone was hungry. They only had coffee this morning, and everyone was too nervous to eat anything, but now they all thought food sounded good. Let's head over to the diner and get some food.

As they were leaving the drug store, Kay walked in with Nick. They all stopped to say Hi. *Kay was an old college roommate of Harper's, she is renting one of the apartments above the store that Harper owns, and Nick owns the Good Time Bar at the corner. She is an author; she is writing her seventh book and needed a change of scenery, so she ended up here in Addison. She and Nick have become an item. Harper will find out all about that some other time.*

Harper stated that they were headed over to the diner for some food, would they like to join them. Nick said, sure. We can catch up with you guys since your vacation.

All of them ordered breakfast food, even though it was eleven-thirty. Harper told Kay she did get to read her first six chapters of her new book, and she wrote a few things on the sides of the pages. Harper hoped she would let her read more. Kay had three more chapters done, she said.

She will get them to Harper as soon as she could. They started talking about their vacation. About the dead guy in the cabin next to theirs. They also inherited a dog from the same place. Liz began to tell them about the housing fiasco. Kay and Nick said. "There is never a dull moment with you guys, huh?"

Harrison had to get to work by three o'clock, and Tom needed to head over to his office and tell his guys about building houses next spring. They all had different places to be so, Liz headed back over to her office. Harper headed home with Harrison. Kay and Nick headed to the town square.

Harper was trying to make heads or tails out of her closet, so Harrison had some room for his clothes. She went through most of her things; she threw a few things away. The rest of the stuff Harper moved to the spare bedroom. She succeeded in rearranging the bedroom to allow for another dresser. Harrison will have to move it over whenever he has the time.

Harper had to go back to work at the Village Restaurant. She told Aaron her boss she would be back in on Tuesday that gave her one extra day to get caught up from vacation.

Harper knew the Garden Girls would be coming in, and she loved waiting on them, plus she wanted to find out what they were going to do with Helen's money.

Harper had so much money that whatever she got from Helen's estate, she was giving it to the Garden Club Girls. Helen used to be one of them until she had to move from her home into the apartment. They planted fruits and vegetables during the summer and took their harvest to the needy. Most of their churches had a list of needy families.

Harrison was not going to get out of work until eleven o'clock, so; Harper had plenty of time to make some more lists.

This time she was concentrating back on the murdered guy from the cabin. As she was writing, she remembered Molly said something to her about keeping Ruddy away from Mr. Jeff because he didn't like him. She wondered why Ruddy didn't like him. I wish dogs could talk. She needed to figure out how she could go back up to the lake and talk to some of the people.

Aggie, Harper's neighbor, stopped over. Harper was telling her about the murder and Ruddy, not liking Mr. Jeff. Aggie told Harper she needed to find out why Ruddy didn't like Mr. Jeff, and here's how Harper could do that.

Chapter Eighteen

Now Harper just had to figure out how to make Aggie's plan work.

It's Tuesday, so that means back to reality. Harper and Harrison both had to work early today. Harper had to work from ten until three, and Harrison had to work from seven am until three.

Harper was glad to get back to work. Especially today because the Garden Club Girls would be coming in for their monthly outing. Harper had the tables all set up for them when they got there around eleven o'clock. Almost all of the girls were here today. "Now if I could just remember all of their names. Let me try; there is Gladys, Terri, Kathy, Kelly, Karen, Debbie, Anne, Pat, Boo, Karla, Susie, Bonnie, and Judy. I think that is all of them. Karen and Judy were not here today. They're sisters, and Karen didn't feel so good today. Of course,

Helen used to belong to this group until she passed away. There have been other ladies; they come and go. They are the sweetest ladies, and I have seen some of their gardens. They are beautiful. No weeds, just lots of strawberries, tomatoes, green beans, and some of the ladies also grow flowers. You name it, and they have it growing."

Harper had to show all of them her engagement ring. They were so very happy for her and Harrison.

Gladys asked Harper if she ever heard about the blue ribbon for the pecan pies from the fair?

Harper told her no. No one ever said one thing about the blue ribbon. She thinks she will have to enter the contest again next year and hope no one dies. Harper asked Gladys if she had heard that Megan Elizabeth Miller was the one that killed Katie Dunlap? Gladys said she had heard that, but it came from Nettie (the head of the busybodies), so she didn't know if it was true or not. Everyone thought it was Missy Jane Clarke, but here Katie Dunlap had stolen Megan Elizabeth's husband, so she killed her for revenge. At least it wasn't Nettie who killed Katie. Nettie's mean and all talk, but she wouldn't kill anyone.

Gladys had a suggestion for Harper. Next month we will be here around the second Tuesday of the month. What do you say you make your Caramel Pecan Pie and us ladies will judge it; you may even get that blue ribbon here instead of at the fair?

Harper thought that sounded great. Now she just had to remember to bake the pie for next month. That was so sweet of the ladies to want to give her a blue ribbon since she didn't get one at the fair.

When Harper finished her shift, she walked over to the drug store to see Liz. But first, she ran upstairs to Kay's apartment to give her back the first five chapters of her new book, and then she could pick up some new ones.

Kay answered the door, and Harper went in. "Here are the first few chapters you gave me to read, and I'm ready for some more."

Kay said. "Great, let me get you another four chapters."

"Wow, the other day, you said you had three more done, and now it has turned into four."

"Some days, the words come easier than other days. And lately, they seem to be pouring out of my brain, which is a good thing. After making the move to this beautiful quaint village, I think I have my eighth book already in my head. You may get tired of reading my books."

"Never, I need to get your other books and read them also. I love cozy mysteries. They're like a Home Mark Movie. Sweet and no bloody murder scenes. But there are so many twists and turns, so you never know until the end who did it."

Harper told Kay how much she loved her characters. Do they stay the same in each of your books? She also really enjoys how you end a chapter. So, you have to turn the page to get to the next chapter to find out what else is going to happen. You do that very well.

"Thank you, Harper, that was very kind of you to tell me that. Some people leave me reviews that are just awful. Others are kind, but the ones that tell me to stop writing are the worst. I've only gotten a few of the hate ones, but they are upsetting."

"Don't you dare stop writing. You are the best author I know, and I love your stories."

"Am I the only author, you know?" Kay laughed.

"No, seriously everyone in the Inspiring Authors Group is an author because we are published in our Anthologies. So, see there, I know lots of authors."

"If you are serious about reading my other books, how about as your pay for being my beta reader I will order and give you one of each of them?"

"Kay, you don't have to do that, I can order them."

"Trust me; I get them much cheaper through the author's discount. Please let me do this for you?"

"If you insist, I would love to read the rest of them."

"You know you should make a book of all of your poems. It is easy and not very expensive."

'No, I could never do that."

"Yes, you could, we will talk about it some more at a later date. Just think about it."

When Harper got back down to the store, her brain was going a mile a minute. Could she do this? She talked to Liz about making a book of her poetry. Liz also thought Harper could do it. Once Harper set her mind to something, there was no stopping her.

Right now, Harper had a full plate. She was getting Harrison moved in and planning a wedding, taking care of a dog. Her job at the restaurant and checking in at the store. There were too many things happening at once. Plus, she still had to find out who killed Mr. Martin.

Chapter Nineteen

Harper had today off, so she has decided to start on the list of things she has to get done. She told Harrison she would go to the courthouse and get Ruddy his license, then take him to the vet and check on his shots. She will go and get him all the stuff they need for him.

- Some toys – lots of chewy toys.

- A bed.

- A leash.

That would be one thing off her list of things to do.

Whenever Harrison has another day off, maybe he can bring a dresser over to put his clothes in.

First things first off to the vet Harper and Ruddy went. They found out Ruddy had a chip in him to say who owned him, his name, and his shot record. Dr. Pett (yes, that is the vet's real name) said it would only take a minute to change the chip and put Harper's name and address on it. His shots were all up to date. Ruddy had already been neutered a few years ago. So that was good. No little Ruddy's running around on Harper's shift. From the vets, they went straight over to the pet store. Ruddy picked out a couple of toys.

Harper picked out a bed and a couple of bowls. Dr. Pett had told Harper, Ruddy could eat dry dog food or from a can whichever he liked best, or switch it up now and then and give his both. She bought a leash because right now, she just had a small rope tied to his collar. While Harper was there, they had a place where they groom dogs. She signed Ruddy up for a bath and a haircut. They were out of there in less than an hour. She also bought him some doggie treats. She gave him one after they left the store. He looked and smelt so good. He looked like a different dog. He even knew he looked better, he kind of strutted out of there.

When they got home, she washed each one of the bowls, and then she filled one of his new bowls with water and sat the food bowl beside it for later. She laid his bed on the kitchen floor, not sure exactly where she wanted it yet. In his bed, she put his toys, a squeaky toy and a rope thing. She had to hide the treats up high in the cupboard.

Harper felt good about so many things off her list.

She headed into the drug store, but first, Harper wanted to talk to Kay about Harper making a book of her poems. How would she go about making a book? She headed up to Kay's apartment. When Harper got to the top of the stairs, she heard Kay yelling. So, now Harper didn't know if she should knock on her door or not. Harper stood outside the door for a few minutes, and the yelling had stopped. She thought Kay was alone, whoever she was yelling at must have been on the phone. Now all Harper heard was crying. It was against her better judgment, but she knocked anyway. Kay came to the door; her eyes were all red from crying; she seemed very upset. When she opened the door and saw that it was Harper, Kay grabbed her and started crying again. "Please come in, you don't know how much I need you right now," Kay said between sobs.

"Kay, what is going on? I heard you yelling at someone."

"Do you remember Pete Johnson from college?"

"Yea, didn't you two date for a while?"

Date? We got married. What a mistake. I can't believe he found me so fast."

Kay and Harper went over to the couch and sat down. Kay went on to tell Harper that after they got married, Pete became very jealous and abusive. If she even looked at another guy, Pete would go off and accuse her of all sorts of things. Then he turned abusive. Pete would beat her up and tell her now no one will want her after he got through with you. She finally got up the nerve to leave him, she did that twice, but he found her each time and would drag her back home. The third time was a charm. She ran so far and so fast she wasn't even sure she knew where she was. She only knew she was away from him.

That is when Kay started writing her books. They are cozy mysteries, but someone always dies in the story. She said so far; she has killed him off in her books seven times. It helps her cope with what a monster he was to her. But now he has found her again. She was afraid.

Harper let Kay know she would do everything in her power to help her and keep him away from her.

Harper told Kay she needed to go down to the store and see Liz for a minute. "While I do that, I want you to pack a bag you are coming home with Harrison and me for a few days. Harrison gets home soon, and we can talk to him and get his advice on how to treat this situation."

Kay was grateful for having a friend like Harper.

Harper went to talk to Liz, and Kay went to pack a few things, even her laptop. She grabbed the last few chapters she had printed off.

Harper told Liz what was going on, but did Liz need anything for the store? Liz told her nothing that can't wait. Just get your friend and get her out of here.

Harper came back up a few minutes later, and she and Kay left together.

When they pulled into Harper's driveway, there was a shiny new truck in the way. Harper said. "I don't know anyone with a new truck. Does Pete have a truck?"

Kay came back with. "I have no idea what he has, but he could never afford a new truck like that."

Harper and Kay went to the back door, and when they entered, they heard voices. Harper said. "One of the voices belongs to Harrison, but I'm not sure about the other one. You stay here in the kitchen until I see who it is."

When Harper entered the front-room, Harrison jumped up and said. "Here's my fiancé. Harper meet Clay Shoemaker; he just started on the police force here in Addison."

"Hello, Clay." We shook hands, and then I said. "That new shiny truck in our driveway isn't your Harrison, so, where is your car?"

"It's still at work deader than a doornail. I'm going to have to call George at the garage and see if he can fix it, or a shiny new truck may be in my future."

Clay started to leave, saying it was nice to meet you, Harper. I hope to see you guys more often. You guys will have to meet my new bride, Penny, one of these days. See you at work, Harrison, sorry about your car. If you need a lift to work, just let me know.

Okay, I will.

Chapter Twenty

Clay left by the front door. Then Harper told Harrison she has Kay in the kitchen. We need your expert advice. They both went to the kitchen. Kay was sitting at the table with her head down. Harper touched her and said. "Kay, are you okay?"

Kay's reply was. "Yes, I'm feeling better."

"Go ahead and tell Harrison what is going on."

Kay started by saying her ex-husband has found her again. She explained to Harrison about Pete's jealousy and his abusiveness. This was the third time he has found her, but she will never go back with him no matter what. She divorced him a couple of years ago. She knows he knows because he had to sign some of the paperwork.

Harrison started asking Kay some questions. "Does he know where you live, or did he just call you because he could get your phone number a lot easier than your address?”

“He just called me and started in on me. When was I going to come to my senses and come back home? I told him to leave me alone. I was not his puppet any longer. He kept saying he would find me, and then we will see about all of that. What am I going to do? He can’t find me again.” Kay now started crying.

Harrison tried to reassure her he was not going to find her and even if he did, she did not have to go anywhere with this lunatic. We need to go down to the police station and get a restraining order against him. So, if he did show up, she could have him arrested if he comes near her.

Harper went over to Kay and hugged her and told her it’s all going to be okay. You’re going to stay with us a couple of days until you get all your ducks in a row. The restraining order, change the locks on her door. When he calls you again, try and get the number he is calling from, and we can have that number blocked from your phone. And whatever else has to be done.

Kay hugged Harper and told her she didn't know how she could ever repay her for helping her like this.

Of course, Harper told Kay you would have done the same for me if it was the other way around.

Harrison said. "Let's go to the police station and get the restraining order in place."

"Harper, I need to use your car if that's okay?

Harper said. "Sure, I'll stay here and start dinner. We'll eat when you guys get back."

Harper was thinking, *what am I going to fix? Oh, I know, I bought everything for a cobb salad. That's what I'll make. She started frying some bacon, and in the instant pot, she hard-boiled a dozen eggs. They eat hard-boiled eggs all week, and it only takes four minutes in the instant pot. She loves that appliance. Then she cut up the vegetables. Lettuce, tomatoes, celery, and some carrots. Later she worked on cutting up some of the lunch meat, the ham, turkey, and chicken. She made her homemade dressing. Harper remembered she bought a loaf of French bread. Dinner was getting done. She made a pitcher of iced tea. They all liked that.* Now she just had to wait for Harrison and Kay to return.

Harper went into the second bedroom where they had just put all of Harrison's things, and she tried to straighten the room up a bit. It wasn't perfect, but it looked presentable. Kay could at least get to the bed. Besides, she was only going to be here for a couple of days.

Harrison and Kay came through the back door. Ruddy started barking until he saw that it was Harrison. Ruddy kind of sniffed Kay for a minute. Harper told Ruddy this is Kay. She is going to stay with us for a few days, so be nice to her. Kay bent down and started petting Ruddy. Right away, he rolled over on his back. He wanted his belly rubbed—what a goofy dog.

Kay asked. "Does he always bark when someone is at the door?"

Harper said. "Only if it is someone he doesn't know."

"Maybe I should get a dog. Are pets allowed in the apartment?"

"Sure, why not. No one has a pet, but I think it would be okay."

"Add that to the list of things to do. Get a dog."

Harrison said. "That isn't a bad idea even though your ex is not going to show up here. But if a dog gives you a sense of security, then do get yourself a dog. Don't get a puppy; they will drive you crazy. But a dog that is a couple of years old would probably be your better choice."

Just then, Kay's phone rang. She jumped. And the look on her face was pure panic. First, look at the number do you recognize it. Kay looked at the phone and shook her head. She didn't know the number. Harrison told her to answer it and try to be calm.

Kay finally pushed the talk button and put it on speakerphone. When she said hello as calmly as she could, Pete started in on her. She started shaking and handed the phone to Harrison. Harrison took the phone and started talking to Pete, telling him. "My name is Harrison Roberts. I'm here with Kay, and I am a police officer. We just got back from putting a restraining order out on you. So, I suggest you leave her alone. If you come within three hundred yards of her, she can call the police and have you arrested. And Pete, you know you don't want her to do that, so stay away. Goodbye, Pete." That is all Harrison said when he pushed the end button. He never let Pete say a word.

"How did you do that? I don't know how to talk to him like that." Kay remarked.

"You don't have to be afraid of him. He is not going to come here and bother you. Because if he does, you have the legal right to have him arrested, and now, he knows it. You saw the phone number, so if it shows up again before we get it blocked from your phone, don't answer it."

Harper told Kay she had started a list for her-

- Get phone number blocked.

- Get a dog.

- Change the lock on her apartment door. *Wait that is something Harper has to do.*

"Are you guys ready for dinner? I made a large cobb salad with all the fixin's. Let's eat.'

Harrison asked. "Do I have time to call George over at the garage. Maybe he can take a look at my car today?"

"Good idea, dear."

When Harrison got off the phone, he told Harper. "George said he would send Benji with the tow truck to pick it up. Then George will call me later with the results."

Kay said that was the best Cobb salad she had ever had. The salad dressing was wonderful. When Harper told her she made it from scratch, Kay said she would love to have the recipe. Harper assured her she would give it to her.

"You know I put a recipe in the back of my books. Would you mind if I shared the salad dressing recipe?"

"Not at all," Harper said.

After the kitchen was all cleaned up and dishes but away Kay said. "Maybe I should go home. Pete isn't going to find me, and even if he does, it won't be tonight."

Harper tried to talk Kay into staying, but she kept insisting she would be okay. Kay then told Harper she was going to call Nick, and he would stay with her. Harper agreed if Nick can stay, then she won't worry about her so much. Some other time you will have to fill me in about Nick. Kay kind of laughed which was good. She promised she would tell her all about her and Nick James.

Harper took Kay home, and Nick was standing outside when they pulled up. I see your knight in shining armor is waiting for you. Call me tomorrow. I will get the locksmith over here to change your lock. On Harper's drive home, she thought to herself. *I am so lucky to have found my knight in shining armor, and I love him so much.*

They both had to work on Thursday. Harper took Harrison to work; then, she will pick him up at three o'clock and go to see George at the garage and get

Harrison's car. George had already called and said Harrison's car was ready. It was a fan belt or something like that.

Chapter Twenty-One

When Harrison opened the door for Harper, she came running at him and gave him the biggest hug and kisses all over his face while saying. "Thank You."

"What did I do to deserve that?"

"You are the sweetest man in the whole wide world. I don't know how I got so lucky in finding you. But I sure am glad. I never want to go through what Kay is going through right now."

"Babe, you never will. I am here to make sure of that. I know you are very headstrong when it comes to investigating murder scenes, but so far, you have figured out who committed the crime, and you have never been arrested or put in jail because of your sleuthing."

Harper was telling Harrison. "Speaking of sleuthing, you are getting pretty good at it also. Come to think of it; you could be a big help with the crime at the cabin. I think I know how to catch the criminal. It will take you, me, and Ruddy. What do you say are you up for one more sleuthing job?”

“You do know how to sweet talk a guy. When are we doing this?”

“Maybe your next day off because we have to go back up to the cabins. But first, I want to make sure Kay has all her ducks in a row. I need to call a locksmith to change her lock. Help her call the phone company to block Pete’s number and go get her a dog.”

Harrison said. “I have Friday off. Is that too soon?”

“No, that sounds great because I have Friday off also.”

The cabins are about forty-five minutes away, so if we start kind of early, we could be back home before noon. That would be great. “I’ll call Johnny Jones, the owner of the park, and see if he can get Roger (Howard Martin’s) brother and Mr. Jeff Henderson to stop by on Friday morning. When we get there, you should call the local police because one of these guys is the killer," Harper said.

"How sure are you that one of these guys is the killer?"

"Ruddy is going to pick out the killer. Besides, when someone killed Mr. Martin, Ruddy was the only one there."

"Oh boy, I'm glad you asked me to come along on this one. I can't wait to see what Ruddy has to say."

"Laugh now, Mr. Roberts, because Ruddy will crack the case."

Harper called the locksmith and gave him the address of Kay's apartment. The man said he could get to it later today. Harper told him that was fine. Then Harper called Kay to get Pete's phone number off of her phone, so she could have the phone company block that number. When Kay answered, she sounded distraught.

"What's the matter Kay," Harper asked.

"He was here last night." Now Kay is crying.

"You didn't let him in, did you?"

"No, but Nick did, then we called the police and, then Nick punched Pete. It all happened so fast. When the police got here, I showed them the restraining order papers I had, and they took Pete away. How did he find me so fast? When am I ever going to get rid of this jerk?"

Harper wanted to know. "Is Nick still there with you?"

"Yes, he won't leave my side—what a nice man. No one has ever treated me like this before. The police said I need to come down to the station and fill out some more paperwork. I just want them to lock him up and throw away the key."

Harper told Kay. "The locksmith will be there sometime today; he will call before he comes out. If you give me Pete's phone number, I will call the phone company and get his number blocked."

"Oh, Harper, Nick did that this morning. He is too good to be true."

"No, trust me, Nick is one of the good guys. What else do we need to do today? Oh, yea, get a dog."

"Harper, Nick, said he would help me pick one out. The dog has to like him also, or we don't get one."

"Actually, that's not a bad idea. Incredible as it seems, my work here is done. I work late today, so when I get off, I will stop over to see your new addition. And I don't mean Nick." They laughed.

When Harper got off the phone, she had to tell Harrison what had happened in the last few hours.

Harrison said. "When I get to work, I'll find out what is happening with dear sweet Pete.'

Harper finished her shift early, around seven o'clock, she when straight over to Kay's to see the new addition.

As she was knocking at the door, she could hear the dog barking. That's a good thing. This dog will protect Kay when Nick isn't around.

Kay came to the door while holding a dog back. Harper put her hand out for the dog to sniff, and then she started petting him on the head.

Kay said. "Harper, I would like you to meet Lacey."

"She's a girl, not a boy; I better keep Ruddy away even though he has been fixed."

"She has also been fixed, so they can just be friends," Kay remarked.

Nick was there again. Harper asked him. "Who is running the bar?"

"I have a couple of good friends, so when I need a night off, they run the place for me."

Kay stated. "I have told him to go home now that I have a dog to protect me, and Pete is in jail. Is he still in jail right, Harper?'

"Yes, I just talked to Harrison, and he said they would release him in the morning with a one-way ticket out of town and a hefty fine. Did the locksmith come by today?"

This whole time Harper had been sitting there; she has been petting Lacey. All of a sudden, Lacey's ears perked up, and someone knocked on the door. She started barking like crazy. Kay grabbed hold of Nick and had this terrible look on her face. Nick told her she was okay; everything is fine; let's see who is behind the door. Nick went over and looked through the peephole. It was Harrison in uniform. He opened the door and held Lacey back. She started sniffing Harrison, then Harrison bent down to pet her. All was well.

Harrison said. "You got yourself a great guard dog. If she wanted too, she could have bitten my leg off. I'm glad she likes me. I like both of my legs."

Nick then inquired. "Harrison, what brings you by?"

"I just wanted to let you know dear sweet Pete will be escorted out of town in the morning, and he has a large fine to pay. He won't be coming back here any time soon, or ever."

Kay was saying. "How am I ever going to repay you guys for all that you have done for me?"

Harper piped in. "You will owe us forever, so don't even try to leave town. You are our friend, and that is what friends do for friends. We love you, Kay, and you are going to be very safe here in Addison."

Nick said. "I second that."

Chapter Twenty-Two

Friday morning, Harper thought, *it's going to be a good day to put a bad guy away.* She and Harrison were on their way to Shadow Lake Camp Ground. Ruddy was in the back seat, not knowing what was going on. He had a significant role in this capture today. Harrison pulled in to the office area. Harper saw Molly standing outside with Mr. Jeff and Roger.

Before they got there, Harrison had called the local police station and asked if they could send an officer over to the campground.

Harper and Harrison got out of the car but left Ruddy inside for a few minutes. Harper wanted to talk to these two before she turned Ruddy loose. She was telling them that she had proof as to who killed Howard Martin. Of course, Mr. Jeff said sure it was his brother Roger and Roger said it was the big bully of the park Mr. Jeff who killed Howard. While they were arguing, Harper went to the car and got Ruddy. He was on his leash. She hoped she could hold him back, so he didn't go off and hurt one of these idiots.

Harper stood in front of the two guys and said. "Who wants to tell me first which one of you killed Howard before I let Ruddy go? You see, Ruddy saw you kill Howard, and he will try and hurt you because Mr. Martin was his master, and you shouldn't have hurt his master."

Roger just stood there, but Mr. Jeff had beads of sweat on his forehead. And he was acting kind of nervous. Harper said, okay, have it your way. "Ruddy, go get the killer."

Ruddy had been barking the whole time, but when Harper let go of his leash, he tore into Mr. Jeff. Ruddy's teeth were showing, and he was growling, barking, and trying to take Mr. Jeff down and biting his ankles when Mr. Jeff started screaming. "Get him off. I'll tell you everything. Just get him off of me."

Harper kept saying. "Say it, or I will let him eat you alive."

"Okay, I killed the old man, NOW get him off!"

Harrison and the other police officer stood there and watched as Harper got her killer. She got Ruddy's leash and told him; you've done your job here. You got the man that hurt your master.

By now, the police officer had Mr. Jeff in handcuffs and was putting him in the patrol car. He thanked Harper for all her excellent work. Since he confessed, he will be going to jail for a long time.

On the drive home, Harrison couldn't believe Ruddy solved the case. Harper told Harrison. "I knew back when we were here; there was a problem with Mr. Jeff. Why did Ruddy only bark at him? There was a reason, and now we know what the reason was. Plus he plays baseball so he has access to a bat. That is what killed Mr. Martin. That is what you told me the police said that first night." Harper told Ruddy, you get an extra treat tonight. Maybe a bowl of ice cream. Ruddy gave out a little bark. Yep, he knows he did good, and ice cream is his favorite.

On the way home, Harper wanted to know when was boating season over? Harrison told her Labor Day is when they start draining the lake. She wanted to see if they could come one last time for this year?

Harrison assured her they could do that. Rent the boat out for the day. "We will have to check our calendars out and see when we can all do this."

Harper repeated. "ALL."

"Well, surely you weren't thinking of going on the boat without Liz and Tom, were you?"

"No, of course not," they both laughed.

It wasn't even noon, and they were back home. After they dropped Ruddy off, Harrison and Harper headed to the diner to grab a burger; then, they stopped over at the drug store. On their way over to the store, they noticed Kay and Nick sitting in the square with Lacey. A light bulb went off in Harper's head.

When she asked Harrison what if we ask Kay and Nick to come on the boat with all of us? Harrison thought that was a great idea. Harper said now we have to ask them, but let's talk to Liz first. I wanted to let Liz know what happened and ask her if she and Tom would be interested in a day on a boat. Liz said she would check with Tom on an available date. Harper also told her they were thinking of asking Kay and Nick to come along.

Oh, Liz, thought that was a great idea.

When they left the store, they checked to see if Kay and Nick were still in the square. They were so they went over to ask them and to tell them to start finding a date that works for them. Please make sure Lacey can come with us too. Ruddy loves the boat.

Then they were off to Harrison's house to get a dresser. This was a perfect day so far.

Harper was looking for her lists. She had a list of everything separated on sheets of paper.

- Her dog list.
- Catching the killer.

- Their wedding.

- Their house.

- Selling Harrison's place.

Now she had to add going on the boat one more time. She can remove the dog list and catching the killer.

- A day trip on the boat with friends.

What should I take for lunch?

- Maybe some wraps.

- Ham, chicken, cheese, lettuce, tomatoes.

- Mustard and mayonnaise.

- Lots of snacks, chips, pretzels.

- Some fruit, grapes, apples.

- Plenty of water.

- Extra bowls for the dogs.

Wait, everyone may have to drive. Six people and two dogs in one car is not going to work. We'll work it out later. We should probably stop at the diner there in town and have our breakfast; then lunch can be much later. We need all the water playtime that we can get.

Chapter Twenty-Three

Everyone looked at their calendars, and it seems like they can go on the boat in two weeks on a Wednesday. A weekday will be a lot easier to get a boat, and there won't be as many people out on the lake. Just the people that are camping.

Harrison called the marina and set up a boat rental for all of them.

They decided to have breakfast at the little diner up by the lake, then get the boat and be on the lake in no time.

Harper made a list for everyone. You know how she is with her lists.

- Wear your bathing suit under your clothes. (Bring a change of clothes to wear home.)

- Suntan lotion.

- Towels, towels, and more towels. (You will go thru them like crazy.)

- Sunglasses.

- A hat.

- Flip flops for the boat.

Harper had her list. She made each of the girls a copy.

- Lunch - wraps, lunch meat, cheese, lettuce, tomatoes, mustard, and mayonnaise.

- Snacks - chips, pretzels.

- Fruit – apples and grapes.

- Dessert – cookies.

- Plenty of water.

- Paper plates, napkins.

- Bowls for the dogs, water.

- Trash bags.

- Rafts, pool noodles.

They figured out the car situation. Harrison and I drove alone because They had Ruddy, the rafts, noodles, cooler, and whatever else Harper could throw-in. Liz and Tom rode with Kay and Nick since they had Lacey Kay's dog. They all meet at the diner for breakfast. *Today is going to be such a fun day. Harper was thinking.*

They were like six little kids, okay, maybe just the girls. But everyone was in such a good mood.

Tom did inquire. "This is not the boat that blew upright; we're going to be okay?"

Harrison gave Tom the thumps up.

Nick looked like a deer in the headlights. "What about the boat blowing up?"

Harrison had to explain. "The outboard motor blowing up next to the last day of their vacation. But Chuck from the marina made it all right. He got us another boat right away. Everything was good."

All the gear was aboard the boat, and off they went. Harrison drove over by the campground first to show Kay and Nick where they stayed. Harper was pointing out their cabin number thirteen and then number fourteen, that is where the murder took place. Poor Mr. Martin.

Kay covered her mouth. Oh, that had to have been very sad. Harper said it was, but look, we got Ruddy out of the deal.

Kay said. "You guys stayed in thirteen? I always thought thirteen was an unlucky number, but in this case, I guess it was fourteen.

Harper had to tell Kay that thirteen has always been her lucky number. Whatever she did, she always wanted the number thirteen. So far, it has worked out just fine.

"Turtle Cove" here they come. They dropped the anchor; of course, Harrison had to tell everyone the story about when the boat was drifting because the anchor had come loose from the rope.

"So, this is "Turtle Cove" what a great spot. I'm like you, Harper. I like it back here; it is calm and quiet. But where are the turtles?" Kay wanted to know.

The guys had the rafts blown up and the noodles in the water. Ruddy was chomping at the bit to jump in, but Harper told him to hold his horses.

Harrison had put in one of those basketball nets things, so the guys were going to play basketball. The girls just wanted to float around and get some sun. The dogs had a ball swimming between the girls and the guys. They all were laughing and having a great time.

Harper admitted. "I'm getting hungry; I'll go back on the boat and get lunch started. When I'm ready, I'll give you all a holler."

When she got on the boat, of course, Ruddy wanted to follow her, but she told him he had to wait just like the rest of them.

It didn't take Harper long to get everything out; she already made up a bowl for Ruddy and Lacey. From experience, she knew once Ruddy ate, he would want to take a nap. This will work out fine. Feed the dogs; then, they can all eat in peace.

Harper had Harrison put Ruddy up on the boat, and she dried him off before he could shake water everywhere. Then came Lacey, she stood there and let Harper dry her off too. Okay, you two were so good. Here is your food. Harper sat their bowls down out of the way of every ones feet.

The gang started making their own wraps. It was fun to see who put what on their wrap. The guys loaded up with meat and cheese, and the girls did lots of vegetables.

After lunch, true to form, Ruddy was taking a nap. Lacey was lying beside him. Look how cute.

Liz was telling Kay and Nick that next year she and Tom were going to rent a cabin up here. They came up and stayed with Harper and Harrison for a day, and one night, it was so relaxing and fun. Maybe all of us could rent a cabin at the same time and have a week of partying.

Harper told them that they had larger cabins with three bedrooms. They could split the cost of the cabin and rent only one boat. How much fun would that be? All of them were nodding their heads. Yes, what fun.

"If we want to stay here next year, we have to get our reservation in soon, or all the cabins will be gone. When we get home, we have to sit down and pick a date," they all agreed.

Until next year!

Dutch Oven Peach Cobbler

2 Cans of peach pie filling or any fruit pie

1 Box yellow cake mix

1 Stick butter – sliced into pats

1 Can lemon-lime soda (7up or Sprite)

*Prepare about 28 to 30 coals, so they are ready to cook on.

-Oil the dutch oven well before starting.

-Pour the 2 cans of pie filling on the bottom.

-Spread the cake mix evenly over top of the filling.

-Spread the pats of butter evenly over the cake mix.

-Pour the soda over the entire mixture.

*DO NOT STIR THE INGREDIENTS!

Close up the dutch oven and place 12-14 coals, spread evenly under the oven. Place the remaining 14 coals on top of the lid.

Bake for about 20 minutes. Then rotate the oven a half turn. Bake another 20 minutes and then check the top of the cake. It should be a nice baked brown color and will have the fruit filling bubbling up through. If it doesn't look done, let it bake another 15 minutes.

Ranch Bacon Chicken Foil Packet Dinner

4 Chicken breast

1 Pound small red potatoes – sliced in half

1 Stick butter – melted

1 Packet ranch dressing powder

1 Cup cheddar cheese – grated

1 tablespoon Italian parsley – minced

Bacon crumbles – cooked and crumbled

Salt and pepper – to taste

*If using the gas grill, set the heat to medium-high heat.

In a bowl mix together the melted butter with the ranch dressing. Lightly spray the foil squares with non-stick cooking spray. Add the uncooked sliced potatoes into the bowl with the butter and ranch dressing. Toss to coat.

Add the chicken breast to the center of the foil—season with salt and pepper on both sides. Add a few potatoes around each chicken breast. Drizzle the remaining ranch butter mixture over the chicken. Close up each foil packet by folding the sides over the top and pinching it closed to make a foil packet. Grill for 30 to 45 minutes. Take off the grill and now add the grated cheese to each packet and place it back on the grill to let the cheese melt. When all done, sprinkle the bacon and minced parsley to finish.

Cobb Salad Dressing

½ Cup olive oil

3 Tbsp. red wine vinegar

1 Tbsp. Dijon mustard

2 cloves garlic – minced

1 Tsp. sugar

1 Tsp. Italian seasoning

Salt and Pepper to taste

Add all ingredients to a mason jar and shake.

Refridgerate after open.

www.ingramcontent.com/pod-product-compliance
Lightning Source LLC
Chambersburg PA
CBHW070818160726
48004CB00001B/321